To Carol:

Enjoy!

The Train That
Vanished

By Steve Schlager

For my wife Sandy
Together, We Can climb Mountains

Acknowledgements

I would like to thank everyone who contributed to my goal of writing a book. Special thanks to the real Bruce Talley, who let me use his character throughout the book. And to Paula Schlager who helped with the editing of this book. You go girl! And a big thank you to everybody who offered suggestions along the way. You know who you are.

Printed in the United States of America

First Printing, 2017

ISBN 9781973167747

Wuzzman Publishing
1017 Meadowlark Drive
Carterville, IL 62918
Kb9adw@gmail.com
(618) 889-3633

www.SteveSchlager.com

June, 1927

The old locomotive belched thick clouds of steam and black smoke descended like a thick, stinky blanket over anybody unlucky enough to be standing near it as the train lurched from its special siding in the freight yards, then past Union Station in St Louis, Missouri. People held their breath as it huffed noisily past, or better yet, they stayed inside the station until it went by. The little train made a run every two weeks, leaving at the same time, on a Thursday night, pulling out at eight o'clock in the evening on its way out of town, then over the huge chain of Rocks bridge into Illinois, sliding past thousands of acres of corn and soybeans and onward towards coal country. The coal companies had mines and miners anywhere coal was to be found and brought up to the surface, but the head offices were located in the big cities, such as St Louis, Chicago and Pittsburg. The "freight" the little train was carrying, was just paper. Paper money. Hundreds of thousands of dollars every two weeks left the corporate offices of the coal companies, to be distributed the next day, Friday, as the miners completed their daily shift at mines in Southern Illinois and Kentucky. The little train made several stops along its route and delivered cash to nearly a dozen mines by daybreak on Friday.

Four times in the past year, the train had been held up. Bandits appeared out of nowhere and stopped the train, shooting it out with the guards and making off with the money. Each robbery was in a different location. Crews and times of delivery were changed, but always the robbers knew where the best places to stop the train were, and make off with the cash. The coal company hired security guards to keep the money safe as the train made its rounds. Twice, some of the guards had been killed. And twice the guards that weren't killed had proved to be part of the gangs that had robbed the trains.

So the coal companies had gone a step further. They brought in The Wells Fargo Security Agency to safeguard their payroll. The first trip was tonight. The agent in charge was Walter Logston, of Carterville, Illinois. Standing slightly over six feet with a slim but ramrod straight build and wavy brown hair that topped his rugged face, he was nearing his thirtieth birthday. He had been recruited by Wells Fargo straight from the U.S. Army and had become a senior agent less than a year before. Wells Fargo had wanted him to stay where he had grown up because he was intimately familiar with the area and he knew of the bad apples that wandered the land and had the potential to cause harm to Wells Fargo customers. He knew all about the gangs in Southern Illinois and was familiar with the train's route and the stops it would make. Wells Fargo had recommended replacing all of the guards with their employees. However, the coal company was hesitant about paying for three agents at once. So, Wells Fargo reluctantly agreed to allow only one agent to ride in the security car. The other two security guards would be in the employ of the coal company on a trial basis. One security guard would ride in the cab with the engineer and fireman, and the other one would stand guard outside the security car on the "Promenade", the covered deck on the back of the security car. Walter Logston would be inside the security car with the big Armstrong Safe bolted to the center of the car. He would keep watch from behind windows covered with bars and also from a raised cupola in the center of the car's roof. Walter had made up his mind shortly after meeting his two guards that they would not ever have made the cut at Wells Fargo. Something about them just made him uneasy. He had a feeling that neither one would have passed a background check. He made a mental note to ask Wells Fargo to question the coal company about making background checks on their guards. They seemed pleasant enough, but the two hired guards stayed to themselves. Still, he had his doubts. He had a feeling that somebody higher up in the coal company staff didn't like the idea of Wells Fargo agents on their trains and was planning to make an example of tonight's delivery. He was nearly positive that the train would be robbed tonight. Was he causing the tension in the air? It was after regular business hours here in St Louis. Since there was nobody at the Wells Fargo office he could call, he was on his own. He had to do something. He was not about to let the money be snatched while he had anything to say about it.

He had arrived at Consolidated Coal Company's headquarters an hour before the money was to be transferred to the safe on the train. That was two hours after Wells Fargo closed their office in downtown St Louis for the day. After introductions were made all around, and he was introduced to the two company security guards who would travel with him, there was precious little time left before the train pulled out. He hurried to the telephone in Consolidated Coal's office and called the only person he could trust. That was his wife.

*   *   *   *   *   *

The security car was a converted baggage car, complete with a sliding side door. It had been sheathed with two inch thick wood sheets on the inside. Bullets might go thru the wood, but they wouldn't have any punch. There was only one roll down window on each side of the bag-gage car, which would make it more difficult for someone to ride alongside the car and shoot thru the glass. A special table was built under each window that would serve as an armrest for a guard to shoot out of. The cupola was also left as a shooting platform so guards could shoot down at robbers. During cold weather, the old pot bellied stove, which sat in the middle of the security car, would sometimes be cherry red, giving off waves of wonderful dry heat. The wood smell would drift thru the car and make travelling a pleasant experience. Tonight, however, the stove sat cold and quiet, not needed as the warm night air of a June evening breeze blew thru the open windows. Walter Logston could feel the tension in the air as the sun dropped behind the hills to the west and the train chugged on into full dark-ness. For the tenth time, he pulled his pistol from its holster and checked it. Everything was fine. The spare cartridges were in his pocket, should he need them, and his shotgun was standing ready against the big Armstrong safe. He wondered how things were going with Emily. She should be getting ready to meet the train. Emily Logston was not quite as tall as her husband but was equally ramrod straight. Her long brown hair flowed and danced around her face as she walked the streets of Carterville, turning heads where-ever she went. She and her dashing husband, the handsome Wells Fargo agent, made quite a couple in Carterville as the little town grew and pros-pered. In 1927, Carterville was rebuilding its downtown after a devastating fire that had swept thru store after store, leaving charred ruins in its wake. So, the city fathers had mandated that all buildings built from now on be made of brick. Besides, brick looked better and more modern.

This night, Emily was not all happy about that call on their brand new telephone in the front parlor. She wished she had somebody to vent her wrath upon, besides her six year old daughter, Eloise. The last thing she wanted to do was sneak out of her home, under cover of darkness, make her way across town, and wait beside the railroad tracks until the train went by and then pick up a bag tossed out by her husband. What if she encountered a derelict or bum? She didn't have a gun. All of this because her husband had some hair-brained hunch. She had a notion to stay at home and tell her husband she fell asleep and missed the train. But she knew she would honor his wishes. She told her daughter she was going to run an errand and would be back in no time. She tucked her daughter into bed, turned out the electric light and closed the door to her daughter's bedroom. She hurried into the master bedroom, pulled off her evening dress and rummaged in her closet for a pair of long pants. She tied her hair up in a bun and stuffed in under a long billed cap, then turned out the lights down-stairs. Their Ford Model A roadster was kept in a shed behind the house. She opened the doors to the shed, then carefully backed their car out of the garage into the driveway, then into the street and turned on the lights as she drove into town.

The drive thru the north part of Carterville was a pleasant one. The streets were empty at this late time of night. She wondered what she would do if she ran into a policeman but there were none to be seen. As she drove along, she passed block after block of new businesses being constructed to replace the ones lost in the fire the year before. There was an air of prosperity in the air. It simply felt good.

Carterville boasted four sets of railroad tracks running thru the town. But the one she was looking for ran from the northwest into town, then straightened out on its way to Energy. Now that was a unique name for a town. Energy! That town was only a few years old and growing like a weed, all because of coal. Mines were opening up everywhere and the whole of Southern Illinois was booming.

On the western edge of town, the train would have to slow considerably to round a tight curve without being thrown off the tracks. A small grassy area by the tracks made a perfect place to throw a bag. Emily Logston's automobile was parked deep in the shadows as she waited for the train. Another auto came into the grassy spot and turned out its lights. It was a coupe convertible with the top down. A young couple immediately embraced and began some heavy necking. It made Emily so nervous watching them and wishing they would go away that she accidently leaned on the horn. The young couple jumped as if shot, and Emily jumped, too. The young couple quickly left the spot. After a few minutes, Emily started laughing. She laughed until her sides ached. Then she heard the train whistle, as it came thru Cambria, a few miles away. She waited, nervously. The train drew closer, the tempo of its huge driving wheels changing on the uneven tracks, causing it to sway from side to side as it slowed down for the curve. Even a small train makes a lot of noise and it was nearly deafening as it went buy. The Security car was not showing any lights at all as the train went by. She could make out the cupola on top of the security car and could envision her husband throwing the bag over the side then waving as the train was swallowed up by the Shawnee Forest. Of course she didn't see a thing except the dark moving bulk of the train as it went by. She got out of her car and walked over to the tracks. There was no moon tonight, so she nearly had to feel her way along. She found nothing. Then she had an idea. She ran back to their auto, and turned on the headlights. There! There was the bag lying a little further along the tracks. She started up the Ford and moved it over next to the bag. She got out and opened the little trunk and picked up the bag. God! It was so heavy! She finally got it into the trunk and headed home. She prayed she wouldn't get stopped by the police on her way home. She had no idea how she would explain the heavy canvas bag. She pulled into the shed and gave a sigh of relief. She hefted the bag out of the small trunk. How could she get it up the steps into the house? She had an idea. She dragged the bag to the side of the house and opened the coal chute door, and pushed the bag into the coal chute. Once inside, she shoveled coal out of the way in the corner and buried the bag, piling it under a half ton of coal like her husband had asked her to. Exhausted, she went upstairs, checked on Eloise, and fell into bed.

The train slowed as it passed thru Carterville, on the way to the first stop on the edge of Herrin, a wide spot in the road known only as "Number 9". But just before the train was supposed to make its first stop, Walter heard a bang that sounded a lot like a gunshot. Unable to leave his post in the security car, he opened a window further and leaned out just in time to see a body tumble off the train into the scrub brush alongside the tracks.

He pulled back inside quickly, not wanting to draw any attention to himself from whomever had just shot the engineer or fireman or conductor. He thought about it. They didn't need the conductor, so it was probably him. They, whoever 'they' were, would need the fireman to shovel coal into the locomotive and the engineer to drive the train.

Just then, the first stop flew by, as the train didn't slow down any. The guards waiting at the whistlestop for their mine's payroll, shouted and waved their arms frantically as the train continued out of sight towards Herrin. Walter leaned out the window and held up his arms to show he had no idea what was going on. Actually, he had a pretty good idea what was happening. And what was going to happen very soon.

He yelled as loud as he could "We're gonna be robbed. Send Help!" He hoped somebody had heard him.

The train continued on thru Herrin, and failed to stop again at the next mine stop. Once more, guards shouted and waved their arms at the train as it kept on going down the tracks out of sight. Now, out in the country, the tracks made a gentle curve towards Marion. Again and again, mines came and went, and the train failed to stop. Rounding a curve, Walter could see that somebody had built a bonfire right on the tracks to try to stop the train, but instead of slowing, the engine ran right thru the fire and kept going. Gunshots rang out and all Walter could do was hide behind the big safe until they were out of range. He couldn't leave the car unprotected, because he knew that, sooner of later, they would be coming for the money. And he would be ready for them. One thing that bothered him was that the train showed no lights and never blew its steam whistle as it roared thru the towns. Anybody wanting to cross the tracks might have been run down by the train if they hadn't seen it barreling straight at them, appearing like a ghostly apparition out of the night.

South of Marion, the train slowed down. Walter thought it might stop altogether but it kept moving. He risked sticking his head out the window again. The night breeze felt good on his sweaty body. Things would happen soon. He just knew it.

The door to the promenade deck on the back of the security car was locked from the inside, and Walter had the key. He heard a scraping sound on the roof, which sounded like someone in boots trying to sneak across the roof silently. He yelled "Hey, you on the roof. Get back to the front of the train, now!"

No answer from above. He hid behind the safe as best he could. Just then, glass from the cupola blew inward from a shotgun blast. Broken glass sprayed the room, and Walter felt his face sting like a hundred bees had suddenly found him. The big old safe took most of the blast. He fired his pistol twice thru the roof. The back door blew open from another shotgun blast. Walter fired again, this time hitting the Consolidated guard as he barged thru the door. But the guard wasn't done shooting. Walter fired again nearly point blank and the guard finally fell down on his side. Walter dashed out from behind the safe and grabbed the shotgun the guard had used, and swung it up towards the roof just as another blast blew a hole in the roof right in front of him. He ran back towards the safe and nearly made it but something like a horse kicked him in the back and he fell down on his face. He didn't black out, though. He dragged himself behind the safe and pulled his pistol and laid it by his side. He touched his shirt and his hand came away bloody. Strange, he didn't feel too bad. He figured he would, soon enough. The second guard dropped down onto the cupola and fired around the corner of the doorway. He missed Walter by a country mile, but it was enough to get Walter's attention. He raised his pistol and shot next to the door. He heard a thud as the guard fell to the floor of the cupola.

Walter gathered all of his remaining strength together and stood up on shaky legs. His vision was blurred but he could see the layout of the car. He headed towards the back door to check on the second guard, and was rewarded with a surprise bullet in the side from the first guard who fired one more shot at the big Wells Fargo agent before he died.

Walter Logston took the bullet standing up, then backed up to the safe. His vision was narrowing down to a tunnel that kept getting smaller, as he slid down the front of the safe. He felt strangely at peace, but in the back of his mind he knew his time had run out. But he had done a good job. The money was safe.

* * * * * * * *

Not long after she and her little girl had eaten breakfast the next morning, someone knocked on her door. The sheriff stood there, with his hat in his hands.

"Miz Logston?"

"Why hello sheriff. What brings you out to my home at such an early hour of the day?"

"Well I gotta tell you, Miz Logston, it's not really a social call. I was wondering." He seemed like he was having trouble with what he wanted to say. "When was the last time you heard from your husband?"

"My husband?" her hand flew to her throat. "What are you saying, sheriff? Has something happened to my husband?" She felt her heart nearly stop.

"Well, no, not exactly. I mean," he started stalling again. "I'm sorry to tell you that the train he was guarding on was ambushed last night, just outside of Herrin. The conductor was found dead along the tracks just outside of Colp, by Number 9. Your husband was nowhere to be found. We're thinking that the train engineer and brakeman were in on the robbery. In fact, the other two security guards are missing, too."

"So somebody ambushed the train, killed my husband and got all the money. Is that what you're saying?"

Emily Logston stared at the old, balding sheriff, who was crushing his hat in his hands. "That's not all of it, ma'am. Not only the money is gone, but the train is missing, too. The whole goddamn train has just simply vanished. We've been in touch with the railroad and it seems the engineer and the brakeman were brand new hires on their first run. Their papers were forged to say they had a lot of experience on another railroad. Which says to me that they were a part of this whole thing. In my opinion, Miz Logston, your husband had no idea what he was walking into when he got on that train last night."

He stepped off the front porch and then turned back to Emily. "If you see ever your husband again, a whole lot of people would like to talk to him." He got into his new Ford police car and left.

As he turned the corner, she sat down on the front steps and stared out towards the highway. In the distance, came the shriek of a train whistle. The world would keep on turning, she knew. But it would be a world without her best friend. She put her head on her knees and wept. Emily Logston never saw her husband again.

Chapter One

Fancy the dog, lay in the shade of the big old pin oak tree in the front yard and watched his two pals play. Mike and Mason Jennings, aged 6 and 7 years old, respectively, played pitch and catch with an old baseball and catcher's mitt their father had. He had shown them how to throw the ball overhand like the big guys did, and also underhand like the girls softball teams did. Their jeans wore the dirt from sliding into the bases in their front yard just like the big guys did on TV.

On this hot summer Saturday afternoon, they played in the shade of the live oak trees lining the driveway of their big old two story house, all the way out to the highway, where they lived just north of town. Cars and trucks zipped by but the boys scarcely noticed them as they played. Fancy, a short, squat beagle, watched the boys play as she always did, with half closed eyes, and tongue hanging out, as she lay in the shade. Elizabeth Jennings, their mom, wiped her hands on the apron she wore around her waist to keep her faded jeans from getting flour on them. She watched the boys from her kitchen window as she made an apple and rhubarb pie for supper. She wiped the flour from her hands, then slid the pie in the oven. It was just another lazy afternoon in a small town in Southern Illinois, about as far from Chicago as could be possible and still be in the same state. "Hey you guys, you want some lemonade?" 'Yeah!" they both said. They dropped their ball gloves and ran for the house. It didn't take long to work up a sweat in the afternoon sun, playing baseball. Lemonade was always a welcome break for a couple of hard hitting players. "Thanks, Mom," each said as they placed their glasses in the sink to be washed as they went back outside. A few minutes later, they resumed play.

Mason wound up his throw and let loose an overhand throw that went wild, smacking the tree and careening down the driveway towards the highway. The boys instantly raced after the ball, throwing caution to the wind as they raced each other to retrieve their dad's ball. "I got it!" yelled Mikey Jennings as he raced his older brother to the ball. The ball rolled out into the middle of the highway. Mason, put his arm out to catch Mikey as they reached the edge of the yard. The boys stopped short of the road, just like they'd been taught. Fancy breezed past the boys, out into the road and grabbed the ball in her powerful little jaws. As she turned back towards their driveway, she never felt car's bumper that cracked her skull and sent her tumbling end over end under the car as it drove on, never slowing down at all. The ball was still clutched in her jaws.

The boys took all this in inside the space of two seconds. The body of the dog lay in the road, unmoving. Throwing caution to the wind, the boys screamed and raced out into the road to their fallen companion.

A truck driver was on his way from the trucking terminal with his last load of the day when he saw the car hit the dog. The car probably didn't have time to swerve or brake, but then again, he was far enough away to take notice of the kind of car, a red mustang convertible, and the two occupants a boy and a girl. Had to be teenagers. At least they weren't very large people. Not like grownups. He'd seen dogs hit before, and there was nothing he could do about a dead dog in the road except try to miss it. Then he saw the boys run into the road and that instantly got his attention as he slammed on his air brakes, cursing and shouting to the boys at the same time "Get off the damn road!" Of course they couldn't hear him, and the semi box trailer got his attention in his mirrors as it started to drift sideways while he tried vainly to slow his big rig. He grabbed the air horn cord hanging from the ceiling of the truck's cab and pulled, hard. The loud horns added to the shriek of the tires as they locked up, laying down a hot smoking line of rubber as he tried to keep his rig under control and miss the boys kneeling in the road just ahead. By the time it dawned on him that he could always take the shoulder, the big rig was nearly stopped. He climbed down out of the truck's cab on shaking knees, said a little prayer, and went to help.

Cars coming from the opposite direction stopped in the road, and drivers got out of their cars to help the boys get off the road. People were milling around in the road, speaking in low tones to each other, as more cars stopped.

"Mason! Mikey! Their mother screamed as she raced down the driveway towards them, the apron around her waist flying in the breeze. She went down on her knees and put her arms around the boys as they told her about Fancy, their little chests heaving great sobs. She buried her face against the boys and wept with them as the truck driver gently picked up the dog and laid him beside the road. A siren in the distance grew louder as a Carterville police car drove around the stopped vehicles and onto the shoulder. The police officer knelt beside Elizabeth Jennings as she sought to console her two boys. A death in a small town always gets everybody's attention, even if it was a small dog named Fancy. The truck driver told the police officer about the red convertible.

"That was a big bump" the girl in the Mustang said dreamily as they sped on. Her eyes were half closed from the speed flowing in her veins. "I dunno what it was. Maybe a rabbit or sumthin," her 16 year old boyfriend said. He was dimly aware of a thump a moment ago. But the car seemed fine, and he wasn't about to stop now, not with his hand inside the waistband of her shorts. She wasn't resisting at all, and he smiled to himself, the incident already forgotten.

Chapter Two

The next day was Sunday, and usually a day reserved for church, eating one of Elizabeth's big home cooked meals, going to a softball game, or DQ, but today was a day of mourning. Nobody wanted to do anything, and Elizabeth didn't push it. She was as heartbroken as her two boys but she wanted them to work thru their grief as a part of growing up. They had a family meeting to decide what to do with Fancy's body and where to bury their beloved pet. Their front and back yard was shaded by several large old pin oak trees, and it was decided to lay Fancy to rest near the back fence, between two of the large trees. Elizabeth would decide what to bury Fancy in.

She wandered thru the house trying to decide what would make a sturdy casket for their little dog. Then she remembered a trunk of her grandmother's. It was downstairs in the basement, nearly forgotten. She went down to the basement, under the big old house. When she was a little girl about the age her boys are now, she would play down there. It was damp and usually chilly, full of rooms piled high with old furniture, boxes of all sizes and a little girl could envision all sorts of witches, goblins, and other fanciful creatures hidden in the gloom and cobwebs of a little girl's imagination.

That was a long time ago; a time when she had a mother and a father and everything was just the way it was supposed to be for a little girl growing up in a small town. But her fairytale shattered when her mom and dad split up and her dad moved away. He never came back, and she grew up without a father, not knowing that she herself would be the mother of two young boys who were growing up without a father, too. She shook her head to try to clear away the past and wandered around the basement, letting her little girl memories flood her mind.

It took a little while to find the trunk she had remembered, but she finally found it. It seemed to be about the right size; not as large as a regular steamer trunk. It was heavy. She had never moved the old trunk from the rafter where it had stayed for many years. Judging from the dust and cobwebs covering the trunk, it had been there for a long, long time. She inspected the trunk from the outside and decided that this one was just the right size for the body of a beagle dog. She carried it over to an old kitchen chair and brushed off the dust on the chair with her hand. She sat down, with the trunk next to her. As she began to open it, she became a little girl again and imagined a 'woosh' as trapped air sprang from the trunk and out came a genie, thankful to be let out of his confines, and ready to grant her three wishes. But nothing happened as she opened the lid and she was transformed once again back to being herself, a grown up mom. Inside, she found a stack of old letters rubber banded together. The writing was a flowing script, probably written with a fountain pen. She read one of the letters and realized they were from her great-grandmother to her great-grandfather when they were 'courting'. The stately old two story house on an acre just outside of town had been in her family since her great-grandmother and great-grandfather had moved in around 1900. They were the first owners of this stately old home. It had been kept up over the next century, first by her great grandparents, then her grandparents, and Elizabeth had no intention of ever leaving this magnificent old home with its beautiful wide front porch, complete with a porch swing. It was a perfect place to spend a summer's evening, waving as her friends drove by. When Elizabeth was a little girl, her mother and father divorced. Then, scarcely a year later, her mother had been killed in a traffic accident out on the big highway that ran thru town. She was taken in by her grandparents and grew up in this house until she graduated from high school and went away to college. Her grandfather died soon after she married. And when her grandmother could no longer live there alone, she gave the house to Elizabeth. The timing had been just right, because Elizabeth's husband had just been caught with the wife of the Methodist minister in the back seat of their car. It made for quite a scandal in their little town, and resulted in two divorces being granted. So, it was easy for Elizabeth to move back into the old house she loved, and her boys loved it there, too, with the huge yard on the edge of town.

She took the letters out of the trunk and laid them on a shelf. Under the letters were newspaper clippings and what appeared to be an old canvas sack. She heard the boys upstairs and laid the clippings on the shelf along with the letters. The canvas sack she dumped onto the basement floor. On the side of the sack was printed Wells Fargo & Company. Whatever was in the sack would have to wait until later. She wiped off years of dust and took the trunk upstairs, and showed it to the boys. They liked it.

That afternoon, she and the boys dug a grave for Fancy and laid him in the trunk, covered up in his favorite blanket. They placed the trunk in the grave and each one said something about Fancy they wanted the others to remember. Then, they each took turns filling the grave. Supper that evening was a somber affair, and nobody wanted to watch a movie or any TV. So, the boys decided to go to bed early.

As she sat in the living room, trying to read a book, she remembered the letters she had taken from the trunk. She turned on the basement light, and went downstairs. The night air in the basement was still and dank as she removed the letters and the clippings and took them upstairs. She spread them all out on the kitchen table.

Her great-grandmother and great-grandfather had not known each other long when they started letter writing. He had been away in the army, thankfully between wars, and had never seen battle. One interesting letter had him trying to explain to her great grandmother the flying machine he had seen with his own eyes. He was really excited. He told her he was convinced that someday flying machines would be everywhere and ordinary people would ride in them. Her great grandmother's reply back to him in another letter told him she thought he was a big dreamer. She said that she would be happy if ordinary people could have automobiles, if ever they were affordable for folks like them. She said she could easily do without horses and their upkeep. This made Elizabeth chuckle. The things they talked about in their letters were a part of world history, and she was amazed at the changes over the years since the letters had been written. In a way, she didn't want to pry into her great grandmother's love life, but it was fascinating reading and she couldn't put the letters down.

After a while, the content of the letters changed. From courting to planning. Elizabeth figured that her great grandfather had proposed and her great grandmother accepted. This was the last time he would write to her. After that last letter, She figured they had gotten married, and there was no need to write.

With the boys already in bed, Elizabeth slipped down to the basement and found the canvas sack. It was quite heavy. She opened the flap and turned the bag upside down and dumped the contents onto the basement floor, and was shocked to find stacks of banded hundred dollar bills. Each was printed with Consolidated Coal Company on the band. She picked up a band of bills and counted a hundred bills wrapped in the band. Ten thousand dollars! In just this band. She coughed, only because she had been holding her breath, as she looked over the money. Was this money from a train robbery, she wondered? How did it get here? Suddenly her mind was filled with questions with no ready answers.

She thought about it for a moment, then realized she knew just where to start asking.

Elizabeth decided she would pay a visit to her grandmother. Her grandmother was now living out her last days in a nursing home in town. She was nearly bedridden, and had fallen several times at home before being convinced to move into the local facility.

After getting Mikey and Mason off to school the next morning, she wrapped up some homemade applesauce bread and headed for the nursing home. Her grandmother was sitting up in bed, reading the newspaper, when Elizabeth arrived.

"Grandma," she said, "It's good to see you. You're looking pretty fit today."

Her grandmother wore a white frilly housecoat over her nightgown, and somebody had done her hair recently. She brightened up and smiled at her only granddaughter as Elizabeth pulled a chair close to her bed and sat down. "I heard about your little dog, poor thing." She laid the newspaper aside on the bed. "I hope you'll find another little dog for the boys. Dogs and boys go well together, you know."

"Especially," Elizabeth thought, "If there's no father around to guide them."

She opened her purse and pulled out several one hundred dollar bills and handed them to her grandmother. "I found this money in the basement," she said. "They were in a trunk in the old coal bin. The dates on them are in the 1920's. They are all one hundred dollar bills. And the stacks are banded with CONSOLIDATED COAL COMPANY printed on them. If I counted right, there's two hundred thousand dollars in that trunk. Is this your money? Where did it come from?" Her grandmother looked as if she had seen a ghost. She gazed into the distance, as if bringing back long ago forgotten memories.

She looked beyond Elizabeth, gazing into the past. "When I was a little girl, my mother would tell me stories about my daddy, your great grandfather. I was too young to remember many things about him. My mother said he was a handsome man, tall and lean. Women took one look at him and just swooned. But he made the right moves on my mother and they were married. He had always wanted to be a policeman, but local police departments didn't pay very much and with the talk of a depression coming on in the next few years, he talked it over with my momma and decided to go to work for Wells Fargo, a growing company out in San Francisco, California. They were opening offices all over the country and looking for guards and detectives, and my daddy applied and got a job working out of the St Louis office. Soon he

was riding a train that delivered payrolls to coal mines all over Southern Illinois, Indiana and Kentucky. He did well, and was promoted
twice in just a year. Now he was a supervisor, but still riding the
trains. She said he really wanted to become a detective. Detectives
were usually really smart, and considered the best of the best in law
enforcement. That's what he wanted to do."

"You've heard of the Shelton gang? And the Birger boys out of Ben-
ton?" Elizabeth nodded. "It's in all the history books around here, all
about "Bloody Williamson County and all that. Daddy was a part of
that?"

Her grandmother nodded. "He was part of the ones that tried to put an
end to the lawlessness that swept through the countryside. It seems
like the local cops just stood aside and let them men stick up banks
and stuff. Then they started hitting on trains. And it didn't take them
long to figure out that the payroll trains carried more money than any
others. Now if the coal miners had been on the trains and the Shelton
gang stuck them up and tried to take their hard earned money, there
would have been a bloodbath like you've never seen. But the coal
companies hired Wells Fargo to make sure the money got delivered.
Well, I guess several trains got held up. That's where your great
grand-daddy got involved."

She adjusted herself in the bed, then went on.

"My daddy got word from a snitch that a train was to be held up on a
certain night. Problem was, he didn't hear about it until the St Louis
office had closed for the day, and there was no way to get reinforce-
ments to help him. He was all by himself. And he had a bad feeling
about the two guards Consolidated had just hired that day to ride
along on the train. And my daddy didn't like the looks of them. At all.
So, daddy made a phone call from the station to my momma and told
her he was going to throw a bag off the train just before the train got
to town, and to take the bag and hide it. When he got back home, he
would retrieve the bag and possibly make some arrests and there
would be lots of publicity for Wells Fargo & Company. Maybe even
another promotion, and they could move from Carterville to St Louis

or beyond. I could tell my momma was excited that they might get to move away to a big city. I think she was fed up with small town ways and all the gossip that went along with living where everybody knows your business."

"My daddy never came home. The train supposedly was robbed, then stolen, and the train was long gone. That train was never found, and neither was your great granddaddy, my father." She teared up, and her voice started shaking: "my daddy just disappeared. I suppose that where ever the train is, that's where your great grandfather is, too."

"My momma never got over him leaving her like that. She loved him so, and I know he loved her just as much. My few memories of my daddy were of him swinging me around and playing tag with me in the side yard. We all laughed a lot. We were a young happy family. He never saw me grow up, or graduate from high school or fall in love and get married."   Then she sighed a big sigh and continued:

"Of course, he wasn't around when my husband and I had our only baby, your mamma, and then he wasn't around to see your mamma grow up either. And now you're following in what seems to be a family tradition of single women with no husband around." Elizabeth's mother and father had divorced when Elizabeth was a preteen. Then a year later her mother had been killed on Highway 13 near Carterville. She moved in with her grandmother and had finished growing up living in her grandmother's house. When her grandmother could no longer care for herself, she gave the house to Elizabeth. And, Elizabeth had had the foresight to have a prenuptial agreement made with her then to be husband, so that in the event of the marriage failing, she would get to keep the house. She was really happy that she'd done that.

Elizabeth nodded, and teared up a little herself. She held her grandmother's hands and they cried together. Three years ago, her happy little family life was ripped apart when her husband, the local high school superintendent, was caught in the backseat of their car, parked in the city cemetery, stark naked, with the wife of the Methodist min-

24

ister. What a scandal that was. The fairy tale life she had built for herself came completely undone.

Elizabeth's grandmother went on: "My mother worked two jobs almost until the day she died, in order to make ends meet. I started working when I was twelve, cleaning houses after school. We did what we had to do, to make ends meet. There was no such thing as welfare or charity way back then, not that my mother would have ever even considered it. I had graduated from school and had just gotten engaged to your grandfather when my momma died. I was all alone. We had no living relatives that I knew of. There was nobody on my side of the church to see me get married. I walked down the aisle all by myself. After we got married, we just moved into the house. Your grandfather was a hard working young man back then, working daylight to dark it seems, so that we could have a good life. He had starting working at the hardware store downtown when he was a young man, and stayed on until he finished high school. A few years later the owner wanted to retire, and he sold it to us. There was so much work to do there at the store, ordering stock and doing inventory and such that we decided that he would work the store full time and I would take care of the house, and work at the store when I could. I think that's why he never found that trunk, or if he did, he never looked inside it."

She suddenly laughed and looked at Elizabeth. "If my husband had ever found that money, I bet he would have fainted! One day, I remembered my momma telling me about the canvas sack downstairs in the coal bin. We had converted to oil years before and there was still some coal left. The coal was still there in a pile, untouched. So, I started digging into the coal. And I found it. What a surprise I got when I opened that old knapsack and all that money fell out! I knew right away that it had to have something to do with the story my momma told me about my daddy and all. So, I figured it must have been stolen. But there was no Consolidated Coal Company around anymore that I knew of. I didn't want to drag our family name thru the mud, so I just stuffed the money into that trunk you found. I liked to never got it up onto the rafters. Then I forgot all about it, until today."

Elizabeth said, "How much money was in the bag? Did you ever count it?"

She said she hadn't. She grasped both of Elizabeth's hands in hers. "The house is now yours. Everything in the house is yours, including that money, however much there is. It certainly wouldn't do me any good, at this stage in my life. Do what you want with the money. But please don't be foolish with it. And, you know, if you suddenly start buying lavish things, people will wonder where you got the money."

Elizabeth had thoughts racing thru her head. It seemed like a lot of money. Her first thought was to buy a college education for her boys. Her grandmother closed her eyes and seemed to be in deep thought for a moment. She suddenly looked at Elizabeth, her eyes a little brighter. "I bet I do know somebody who would know what to do with this money. He's right here in Parkview. His name is Bailey. Howard Bailey. He used to run the old Carterville Savings and Loan before they merged and became a bank. That was a long time ago. Old Howard's hobby was Carterville history, and if anyone would know what to do, it would be him."

Chapter Three

Elizabeth left her grandmother and wandered down the hall, looking for Howard Bailey's room. He was not in his room, so she went to the recreation hall and found several elderly men sitting in a sunny atrium, most of them asleep. One old man was dressed in a white linen suit and white shirt, and sporting a blue bow tie with white polka dots in it. He put down his newspaper and smiled at her. She asked him to point out Howard Bailey. He pointed to himself. "Do I know you?" he asked.

"My grandmother is Eloise Sparks. She lives here, too. She said you might be able to answer some questions I have about Carterville from many years ago." He gazed past her and his eyes seemed to adjust to the light coming in thru the windows. He pointed to a chair. "Bring that chair over here. Now, what do you want to know?"

"Well, I live in the house my grandmother used to live in when she was first married. The big gray house just north of town on the west side of the road."

"Oh, yes," he interrupted, pointing a boney finger in the air, "that house has been a part of the countryside before Carterville was much of a town. In fact, the road out of town towards Colp was just a dirt track until around the late 1800's. It got pretty messy around there when it rained for several days. Seems to me that there was a building date carved in one of the blocks of the foundation if I'm remembering correctly."

Elizabeth said, "You're right!" I have seen that date. It's 1896." An orderly was absently dusting furniture nearby as Elizabeth began speaking.

"Eloise Sparks. Her husband was Bernie Sparks. Nice fellow. As I recall he worked at Cox's Hardware store when he was a kid, and then bought the store from the old man when Rupert Cox wanted to retire. Did all right for himself and your grandmother. Then his eyes got big. "That house didn't burn down, did it?"

"Oh, no, nothing like that," she said quickly. "It's just, well, I found an old trunk, about this big," she gestured with her hands, "and it had some money in it." She dug into her purse and brought out several packs of hundred dollar bills and handed them to him. "You can see that it says CONSOLIDATED COAL COMPANY" printed on the bands. I was wondering how this money came to be in my basement? I think I know how it got there, but now, what should I do with it?"

She noticed the orderly staring intently at the packs of money in her lap. "Excuse me, but we're having a private conversation here. Do you mind leaving us alone?" The orderly mumbled he was sorry and moved across the room.

Howard Bailey turned the bills over in his hands and looked closely at the markings. He stared past Elizabeth into the past. Presently he looked at her again. "Tell me how you think it got in your grandmother's basement."

Elizabeth recounted the story her grandmother told her about her great grandfather being a Wells Fargo agent, and how he wanted to thwart the robbery by hiding the money somewhere else before the bandits got to it. Of course, he didn't plan to disappear into history without giving it back and bringing the bad guys to justice.

Howard Bailey said, "How much money did you find? Have you counted it?"

She nodded. "There's uh, two hundred thousand dollars, all together."

The orderly tripped over a piano bench nearby, and mumbled something like, "Excuse me, I'm sorry." He left the room, limping slightly.

She motioned for him to continue.

"Back in the 1920's there were lots of coal mines around here. And right around here close by were several large mines, employing hundreds of men. That created a big payroll. Every week, a train would come down out of St Louis carrying that payroll, for several of Consolidated's mines." He spread his hands. "Not a big train. Just an engine, a coal car and usually one or two other cars, one with the money in it and maybe a sleeping car for the two or three men guarding the money on the train. In today's dollars that two hundred thousand you found would be probably somewhere around two million or so. This was in addition to all the trains leaving the mines full of coal. The tracks around Southern Illinois were busy all the time, night and day. One Friday morning real early, a payroll train was robbed somewhere before it got to Herrin. I think it was just west of town, but that's just a rumor. However, the train just disappeared. Nobody ever saw that train again. Or the money, either. The conductor was killed. The engineer and the fireman were never found. My guess is they were part of the holdup gang"

"What do you think happened to the train?" said Elizabeth.

"My opinion? I haven't a clue. Pretty hard to make a train vanish into thin air." Howard Bailey looked like an old professor in a classroom. He adjusted himself in his chair and continued on with his story. "A lot of folks thought the trains would be easy pickins' for the money, so every now and then a train would be held up. I know of at least two trains that the Shelton and Birger gangs held up. Your grandmother was just a little kid when this was all going on and her daddy was long gone before she was old enough to know anything about him being a lawman."

Elizabeth said, "You're about the same age as my grandmother. How do you know all this stuff?"

Howard said, "Southern Illinois history is my hobby. Lots of things have happened in this little part of heaven."

Elizabeth said, "What do you think happened to my great grandfather?

"Well," Howard Bailey said, "I heard a rumor that your great grand-daddy got wind of what that gang was going to pull off, and he was going to try to head them off all by himself. But, I guess that didn't happen. That's why he never came back to your grandma and her ma. He was really sweet on them. I don't think he would have just gone off and left them on his own.

"What are you going to do with the money?"

Elizabeth looked at the money, then back at Howard Bailey. "Well, I could give it back."

"To whom?" said the old man.

"I, well, I don't know," she said. She had no idea who to give the money to. She looked around the room, absently noting that the orderly was gone."

Let me tell you about this money," said Howard Bailey. "Back in the twenties, coal companies were making a lot of money off the backs of miners who got paid very little and never seemed to get out of debt. Thus the advent of the 'company store'. The miners would buy what-ever they needed at the store and run up a tab. Then, when they got paid, they settled up with the store. Usually, by payday, they still owed more than what they earned. So, if a payroll train got robbed, the money was replaced right away by the coal company because most miners were living from paycheck to paycheck, and for a bunch of miners to miss one paycheck would cause a mutiny like you've never seen before. Now, this money here, came from the Consolidated Coal Company. I know that they were robbed at least twice during their existence. However, that was a long time ago, and they've been out of business for a long time. They simply shut down, like a lot of coal mines did back then. They didn't sell out to a competitor, because the coal seam they owned just played out. No more coal to mine, so there was nothing for a competitor to buy. Mines were opening and closing right and left back then. They do that even today, when a coal seam runs out. That's the way it is in the coal business. Nothing lasts forever."

Elizabeth looked at him. "What should I do with the money?"

"Short version, keep it. It's your house, you found the money, and the people it was stolen from are dead and long gone. Do something useful with it. Fund your kids' college education." He laughed. "Wish I had a pile like that when I was a young man."

She said, "I really should give it to somebody. It's not right to keep it."

"My dear young lady," he stopped to cough a couple of times, "Carterville is a nice little town. In the interest of self-preservation, namely yours, I think you should just keep it, and not say another word about it, to anybody. However much money there was taken, it is not going to help anybody now, since it was so long ago, and would only stir up old wounds among the townsfolk who had relatives involved. The coal mines are all long gone, their owners and stockholders are all long gone, and I think it would be best if you just kept it and didn't say a word to anybody about where it came from. It would be our secret. I can help you invest it if you like. If you take it to the bank in one big lump sum, they're going to want to know where it came from. It's a federal requirement. If you want to put it in the bank, we need to discuss how to go about doing that so as not to raise any eyebrows. I would first suggest a safety deposit box. But, there is one thing I just thought of that might make a difference." They hadn't noticed the orderly nearby again, polishing the piano furiously.

"I am thinking that this money, which was printed in the 1920's is worth more to collectors that to the bank. In other words, I bet you could sell this currency on e-bay for possibly double what the face value is." Elizabeth gasped. Howard Bailey continued, "You might want to have some of those bills appraised by a reputable currency house, probably in St Louis."

31

She said "Let me think about that. Maybe that would be best for the future."

Elizabeth thanked him and left the nursing home, more confused than ever. As she left the parking lot, she remembered she needed to buy some groceries, so she drove to the Carterville Superette. She wandered the aisles, without a list, and filled her cart with what she thought the boys would like for supper the next few nights.

She was looking at Macaroni boxes when she turned a corner and ran into a man, arms full of cereal and milk, with his back to her. "Oh my gosh, I'm so sorry. I should have..." She looked at the man she nearly ran over with her cart, "Dan Flatt, is that you?" She stared at the man with dark wavy hair, the man she had a crush on when she was a teenager. This was the man whom she let slip away only to return in her dreams once in a while. He grinned. "Well, Beth Anderson, I'll be... wait, it's not Anderson any more is it?" he smiled at her, his eyes dancing over her face.

"No, it's Jennings, but it's not Jennings, it's, I mean, well, I'm divorced. She took a deep breath. "I sound a little stupid, huh?" She got the feeling he was looking at more than just her eyes.

"No, you sound just fine to me. I think you're the first person I've run into, no pun intended," he laughed, "since I got back to town. This placed has changed a lot in some ways and hardly at all in others."

"Are you visiting your mom?" Elizabeth asked. He nodded. His mom lived alone in the house he grew up in, not far from downtown.

"I had some time to kill between jobs, so I thought 'd come back here for a few days and fix some things around the old house. Just got in a couple of hours ago. Mom needed some things, so here I am. She can't do much because of her age, and has let some things go around the house. So, I'm going to have my hands full for a few days. One day I'll be a painter, the next I'll be a carpenter, and the next I'll be a plumber. Yuck, I'm not looking forward to plumbing chores. So, here I am," he said, grinning. They stood staring at each other for what seemed like five minutes, then, Elizabeth said, "Look, I've got to get home and fix supper for my boys." She held out her hand. "Welcome back to Carterville. Maybe I'll see you again sometime, Dan."

Elizabeth piled the groceries into her car and climbed in, and sat for a moment, thinking about Dan Flatt. The young man she had dated when she was a junior and he a senior was back in town. She thought he was a nice enough guy back then, but here he was, an adult, back in town, very assured of himself, and not bad looking either. When they dated, he had just earned his pilot's license and was crazy about airplanes. One summer, he had assembled an ultralight airplane from spare parts and had taken her flying on numerous occasions. When her friends went on dates, they usually went to movies. But when Dan and Elizabeth dated, sometimes they went to movies but often they went flying. They had a lot of fun skimming the treetops, chasing deer and in more than one instance, had landed in a farmer's hayfield to have a very romantic picnic lunch. Those were great, if not distant memories. She wondered if he remembered. Elizabeth carried the groceries into the kitchen from her car and closed the door behind her with her foot. She set the groceries on the kitchen table and began to put things away. Her mind was reeling from the talk she'd had with her grandmother, then Howard Bailey, and then, running into her old boyfriend, Dan Flatt. He had certainly changed, and in her mind, for the better. She had not thought about Dan for a long time.

Dan graduated a year ahead of her and went off to college in another state. The letters between them had gradually grown to a trickle, then stopped when she left for college.

The orderly observing Elizabeth and Howard Bailey was a skinny young man of twenty by the name of Junior Gulledge. For as long as he could remember, Junior Gulledge had been broke. Everyone else had money to spend, but opportunity seemed to pass Junior by. Jobs came and went and Junior just couldn't seem to hold on to one very long. Fridays were paydays, and by Monday morning, Junior had started borrowing from his friends, having had more fun in a weekend than most guys would have all week. Thus, every Monday began a cycle that Junior just couldn't seem to break.

This stupid job at the nursing home was all he could find, and it didn't pay very well. Besides, few guys his age wanted to be seen giving old geezers a bath or emptying their bedpans. The smells in parts of the nursing home made a guy want to gag. You got used to it some, but still...

Then today this young woman sits down with Howard Bailey and Junior thanked God for giving him exceptionally good hearing. She was nice enough to look at, but when he heard her mention money, he was all ears. He heard 'hundred dollar bills', then he thought he heard 'two hundred thousand dollars', and decided to polish the furniture in the room a little better.

He'd seen her around town, and knew she lived here, but didn't know where. After she left, he wanted to race out to the parking lot, jump in his old truck and follow her home. But old lady Winston, the assistant director of nursing, chose that moment to march her considerable bulk into the lounge and chastise him about the amount of time it was taking him to clean the dining room and remind him that he was needed to help prepare the tables for the evening meal which would take place in less than an hour.

"Yes ma'am, I'll get right on it. It'll be done on time, I promise." He sneered at her back as she stalked away. He hoped that one day she would slip on a banana peel or something and break her neck. One could always hope.

Dan left the IGA and headed home with his mom's groceries. As he started to turn on the radio, he felt his phone vibrate with a text message. He tuned in a local country station and breathed a happy sigh as he drove home. His mother had always been one of those healthy happy women who didn't let advancing age slow her down very much. Now in her eighties, she was only too happy to have her only son drop in for a visit. She had made a list of "chores" for Dan to take care of whenever he came by for a visit. Dan didn't mind. He enjoyed fixing things around her house. It was ok living by himself, and most of the time it was ok being a bachelor for the most part, but Dan often wondered how it would be to have a wife and kids, a house to come home to, instead of an apartment. Then, there was his job, being an airplane repo man, along with his pal CJ Rodriguez. He and CJ were completely different but they were great friends. Where Dan enjoyed what little quiet time he could get, CJ lived for fast cars, bright lights and faster women. Dan was tall and slender, where CJ was a short round jolly man of Cuban extract. When Dan got angry, he became very quiet, whereas CJ, on the other hand, started spouting words off in Cuban like a machine gun.

He set the groceries on the kitchen table, stuck his hand in his mother's cookie jar for a couple of homemade chocolate chip cookies and sat down on a lawn chair in the back yard. His mom made the best homemade cookies. It didn't matter what kind they were, all of hers were mouth watering. Then he remembered his phone vibrating and retrieved a text message. This one was from the company he worked for. He punched up the number to return the call.

"Got some work for you, Dan," said his boss. "This one is big money for us. An eight passenger jet. Cessna Citation. The company we made the loan to has defaulted on the loan. Looks to me like they might be going under. We have heard thru confidential sources that they may try to sell the plane overseas. If it would get into the hands of one of the third world countries, we'd never be able to get it back. They'd just laugh at us. We called the loan a month ago and they won't return our calls any more. So, we want you to go get the plane. Last report had the plane based at a small airport in North Carolina. I'll FEDEX you what we have, along with a duplicate set of keys to the jet and see if you can get it back for us. OK?" Dan hung up. Then he forwarded the text message to CJ.

When FEDEX knocked on his mother's door the next morning, Dan was hard at work repairing some soffit at the back of the house. He had ripped off the old weather beaten stuff and was about to put up new vinyl soffit. His mother brought the package from FEDEX out to him. "Here it is, Danny. The delivery man just left." Dan wiped his hands on a towel and sat down at a table on the covered back porch. He loved this part of the house. It was a place where they had often eaten breakfast when he was growing up. Inside the package was a USB thumb drive containing electronic logs for the plane, keys for the jet, photos of the owners of the corporation that had purchased the plane and copies of the loan papers. Dan let out a soft whistle. Twenty eight million dollars. No wonder the bank was worried. The Cessna Citation was a plane that he was certified to fly, having taken a Flight Safety course several years ago, courtesy of the bank. He studied the materials from the FEDEX package, then made some phone calls to the FBO in North Carolina where the jet was. By twisting the truth some-what, he learned as much as he need to know about the airplane he would attempt to steal.

Chapter Four

Ten seconds after his shift was over and he'd clocked out, Junior Gulledge slipped past several orderlies chatting on their way out the back of the nursing home and quickly walked across the parking lot to his old beat up Chevy pickup. He had to slam the door twice to get it to stay closed. It started with a noxious cloud of fumes that rolled out from under the truck and thru holes in the floor that rust had made. It was mainly for that reason he drove with the windows down. A new muffler would have helped tremendously but mufflers cost too much, and besides, choosing between a new muffler or beer? No contest. A muffler could wait. He was thirsty. He drove to the liquor store and left with a twelve pack.

His best friend, a tall gangly young man of twenty was Donald Etheridge, but everybody called him Peanut. Nobody knew where the nickname came from. It fit him and besides, he liked it. Peanut's home was an old trailer in a mobile home park on the south edge of Carterville. The paint had faded many years ago to a sort of turquoise and white design. Scraggly bushes adorned the front of the trailer on either side of the black wrought iron steps. He opened the door and Junior Gulledge pushed past him and shoved the beer into the fridge. He took out two cans and handed one to Peanut. Then he flopped down on the sofa.

"Tough day? Said Peanut, studying his friends face.

"You know, same old shit, different day." Junior had been laying back against the sofa's cushions, but suddenly sat upright. "However, I need to talk to you about something. Maybe things could change for us."

"How so?"

"I overheard some people talking today about some money this chick found hidden away in her house. I heard two hundred thousand dollars. And this lady said she 'just found it!' "

Junior jumped up, nervously pacing about as he talked, pausing once in a while to take a swig of beer. "She was asking advice from old Howard Bailey, the guy who used to run the bank. Now there's a first class asshole. He turned me down for a loan more than once. Not once did he ever give me a chance. It was always 'well, son, you don't have a good enough job,' or something like that. And today, I overhear this chick say to him, 'Oh Mr. Bailey, what should I do with all this money?'. She actually said, 'Maybe I should just give it all away'. I nearly wet my pants. I wanted to run over to her and say 'Please, ma'am, all I need is just twenty thousand. That would buy me a nice truck. You can keep the rest.' Then she turns to me and says to me "Excuse me, but we'd like some privacy here." He looked at Peanut. "That's when she pissed me off." His eyes narrowed. "I say we help ourselves to some of that money."

Peanut looked at him over his beer can. "That's where you're wrong, Junior."

Junior's eyebrows narrowed. He said, "What do you mean? We shouldn't go after that money?"

"No," said Peanut," You said we should help ourselves to some of that money. I say we help ourselves to ALL of that money."

"Yes!" They high-fived, then each helped themselves to another beer and began planning.

Later that evening, they drove around town. Junior had heard old man Bailey talking about the old gray house north of town, and it only took a few minutes to figure out which gray house it was. Lights were on at the house. A White Toyota sedan was parked in the drive. They drove further north of town, then turned around and went back into town, exploring all the roads nearest the old gray house. They decided on

James Street. It would be the closest street to the back of the house. It was a side street that saw very little traffic during the day. Peanut and Junior talked about breaking in to the house together, but Peanut was busy for a few days, so Junior decided he would give the house a try by himself.

The next day, on his lunch break, Junior drove past the gray house again and the white Toyota was gone. After he clocked out at 3 pm, he drove by again, and the driveway was empty. He found a place to park where he could watch the house. A few minutes after five o'clock the white Toyota pulled into the drive. By seven o'clock, Junior's stomach was driving him crazy. He pulled out of his parking spot along the Colp Road and drove thru Hardee's. With a king size sandwich, fries and extra large Coke, he drove back to his parking spot and waited until nine o'clock. The Toyota stayed put. He drove to Peanut's trailer and they decided how junior would proceed.

The next day, Junior called in sick. A few minutes past nine o'clock, he drove past the gray house and the driveway was empty. He drove to James Street. By looking between two houses on James Street, he could see the back of the gray house. He drove around the block and saw nothing moving. He figured most of these houses in this neighborhood were probably occupied by younger couples that both worked. The neighborhood was peaceful and quiet. He drove around town for a few minutes, then went back to James Street and parked. He quickly hopped out of his truck and stuck a crow bar down his pants leg. He walked casually between the two houses and thru the back yard of the gray house up to the back porch. Skirting the porch, he selected a basement window and easily pulled the window out of its frame without much noise.

Across the street, an old man peered out of his living room window at the pickup truck that had parked down the street. With nothing better to do, Sam Henderson kept his favorite chair positioned next to the window so he could keep track of the comings and goings on in his neighborhood. His oxygen bottle hissed gently in the corner of the living room, the long thin green tubing snaking across the worn floor towards his chair. He was resigned that the bottle would follow him around until the end of his days. He had seen the truck go by the first time, and he watched as it slowly drove down the street and turned at the corner, the way someone will drive if they're looking for an address. It came back again a few minutes later, and parked. Just like on TV, the young man slid out of the truck and looked around slowly, then reached back into the truck and pulled out something and put it in his pants. That got his attention. It was just like on TV. Only this was real life in little old Carterville, IL, USA. Sam got his cellphone, took a few deep sucks on his oxygen, then ambled out his front door and scooted across the street. He decided that if the driver of the truck came back, he'd just keep walking down the street. But he didn't return. Sam walked between the two houses across the street from his, and rounded the back of one just in time to see the young man enter a basement window on the gray painted house in the next block.

"Hot damn! A burglar," Sam thought. He turned around and hurried back to the safety of his living room, his chest heaving and his breath wheezing mightily. It took him a minute or two to control his breathing so he could call 911, which he did. He explained who he was and his fears that a house was being broken into. Within a minute or two, a patrol car showed up on his street and stopped behind the pickup. Sam went out onto his porch, trailing the oxygen cord, and yelled at the officers "Hey, I'm the one who called it in." He pointed across the street with his cane. "That guy is still in that gray house on the next block." The officers waved at him and yelled back, "Stay there, we'll want to talk to you in a few minutes."

The two officers walked between the houses but stopped before showing themselves to the back of the gray house. Sam reached up on a shelf in the dining room and pulled down a pair of binoculars in a tattered old leather case. He adjusted the binoculars to his eyes and parted the curtains so he could see but still be mostly hidden. He could just see the corner of the gray house but not the basement window where the man had gone in. Well, Sam had all day. He could wait. He could wait for days if he had to. What else did he have to do?

Junior Gulledge easily opened the basement window and slid inside. He dropped about four feet onto a workbench and then eased himself to the floor. The basement was lit by enough light from nearly a dozen windows that he could see some things without turning on a light. But he turned one on anyway. He nosed around the basement, opening boxes and peering inside sacks, looking into what used to be a coal chute, now empty, and another small room filled with empty glass canning jars. Some furniture was stacked up in a corner, setting up on two by fours to keep them off the old concrete floor.

He crept up the stairs, listening for signs of a dog or any people, and heard nothing. He started with the bedrooms and looked thru each dresser drawer, then every closet shelf. By the time he was through with what was evidently a children's room, he was tired and frustrated. He had always heard on the cop shows that an average burglar was inside a house for just a couple of minutes. He had found nothing. He was upset that he would come away empty handed. He couldn't even find a cookie jar in the kitchen with a few dollars in cash in it. It was time to go. Past time. He started towards the kitchen door, then stopped dead as a dark blur moved past the window. His blood pressure spiked as he slightly drew back the curtain to find two cops watching the back door, both with shotguns at the ready. Shit! Somebody had seen him. Shit! Now what to do? He tiptoed to the front of the house and not only were there more Carterville cops, the county cops were there and there was Illinois State Police as well. He hadn't heard a thing, and here they were, waiting for him. He had never seen so many big guns, and they were all pointed straight at him, and him only. Just waiting for him to make a wrong move, like he had a gun or something and they would all cut loose. His mouth dropped open, and wouldn't close. He couldn't catch his breath. He felt like a wounded fish being drawn ever closer toward the boat. No place to hide, no place to run. Well, goddamn it all. He opened the door slightly and yelled "I'm coming out! Don't shoot me!

Chapter Five

Elizabeth was grabbing a quick cup of coffee from the hospital cafeteria when she heard her name being paged. Blood rushed to her head when she learned that her house had been the scene of a burglary and the cops had already caught the man who broke into her house, at her house. She gathered up her belongings and raced to her car, then drove home. At least five police cars were still there. She parked in the drive and a young Carterville cop she knew came up to greet her.

"Miss Jennings, I'm sorry this happened to you, but at least we caught the guy. We've already got him downtown in jail, so you won't have to I.D. him. What we'd like for you to do is check each room and tell us if anything is gone. We didn't find a single thing on him when he came out of the house, but he could have stashed something somewhere, in hopes of coming back and retrieving it. If you would help us and check please, we'd appreciate it."

She said she would go thru the house with a detective, and together they went from room to room examining each for missing items. She could find nothing missing. They had her fill out a report of a burglary and sign it. One of the cops she knew volunteered that the 'perp' was a young man named Junior Gulledge. When they said he worked as an orderly at the nursing home, she was pretty sure she knew who he was. He was the orderly who tried too hard to clean the furniture near where she was talking with Howard Bailey.

She sat down on the porch swing to wait for her babysitter to bring the boys home. She had developed a huge headache in just the last hour, and she massaged her temples to help ease the pain. It was then that she knew what the burglar was looking for. She raced back to her car and looked in the trunk. It was still there in the CONSOLIDATED COAL COMPANY knapsack. She had forgotten to put the money back in the house after taking it to the nursing home.

The sitter arrived a few moments later to drop off her boys. She was a large, older woman, with frizzy hair, wearing shorts and a polo shirt with 'Cheryl's Kids Kare' embroidered on the left chest.

"Liz, what's going on here?" Cheryl asked. Mason and Mikey crowded around Cheryl and Elizabeth, but both boys were fascinated watching the police. This was real life, right in their own yard. Elizabeth told them all about being broken into. The boys were excited with the news and all the police there, asking questions. Elizabeth decided to keep mum about the money in her trunk. "This is just like on TV!" said Mason. "Yeah, and we're in the program!" said Mikey. The police took notes and a few fingerprints, then walked her through the house, again, room by room. A while later, they left. "You sure you'll be all right?" said Cheryl. "I could keep the boys overnight if you'd like. It would be no problem, really." Elizabeth said no thanks and Cheryl left. It was suddenly very quiet at their house. She made supper for the boys and they watched TV together until eight pm, when she shooed the boys off to bed. She sat down at the kitchen table, and opened a bottle of red wine and poured herself a glass. She held her head in her hands, running her hands thru her hair, then lifted her glass and toasted her reflection in the oven door. "Cheers, deary. Now would be a nice time to have a man around again, ya know?" The next day, after work, Elizabeth went to the hardware store and asked about having new locks installed on her doors and windows.

"Can't help you there missy," the store manager said, "Carterville hasn't had a locksmith in years, and I know there are some in Marion and Carbondale, but I don't know them. You'd just have to pick one out of the phone book.

A voice behind her said "I could probably put them on for you."

She turned around to find Dan Flatt standing there, hands in his jeans pockets. He gave her a lopsided grin and said "I charge, you know. It would probably cost you a dinner sometime. If you're interested." The store manager grinned knowingly at both of them and walked away.

She said, "That's really nice of you Dan." He had the same lopsided grin on his face she'd fallen for when they were in high school together. "But I thought you were busy with your mom's house?"

"Well, yeah I am, but that's an ongoing project, and besides, I was wondering how we could see each other again, and bingo! This just worked out. Why do you need new locks?"

She told him her story about last night and being so scared after the police left that she had spent the night with her dad's old shotgun next to her bed.

"Maybe I should get another dog," she said.

"That would probably be a good idea," said Dan Flatt. "You get the locks, and I'll be over this evening and install them. Say, around six o'clock?"

"Six would be fine, and bring your appetite. Remember, you still have to meet my two little protectors" He waved at her as he left the store. For the first time in months, she felt better for herself. She headed home thinking of what she could fix for a meal. She had all the fixin's for a meatloaf. Men always seemed to eat a lot and she wanted to have enough. Maybe even make a desert. The boys would love that.

Dan Flatt showed up a few minutes before six and rang the doorbell. As he waited on the front porch, he mused about how little things had changed around this house since he and Elizabeth were dating years ago.

The paint seemed to always be peeling from around the windows and the big old front porch still had the loose boards that would creak and groan when you stepped on them (they did fifteen years ago and they did tonight), and the porch swing still hung on the end of the porch, as inviting now as it did then when they had to be careful that her grandmother wouldn't look out the window at the wrong time.

Elizabeth appeared at the door just then, looking radiant in shorts and t-shirt and barefoot. Behind her were two little shadows. "Boys, this is Mister Flatt. She put her hand behind the shortest shadow and shoved him forward from behind her. "Mikey, say hello to Mr. Flatt." Mikey stuck out his hand and Dan shook it firmly. Then Mason did the same with a little less urging from Elizabeth. Mikey was definitely the shy one. "Tell you what, guys, I don't like to be called 'Mister', so why don't you both just call me Dan, ok?" That went over well with the boys and Dan caught Elizabeth trying to hide a smile as she guided everybody into the kitchen for supper.

"Do you still like meatloaf like you used to?" she asked, as she sat down at the end of the table.

"I definitely liked your meatloaf," he said as he sat at the opposite end of the table. The boys looked from Elizabeth to Dan, and then they all held hands and said grace. After that, the meatloaf was divided up and eaten, along with potatoes, green beans and coleslaw and iced tea.

Dan pushed his chair back from the table and said "Man, I haven't eaten like that in a long time! Now I need to get to work to earn that supper."

She showed him the door locks she had purchased; he brought a bag of tools in from his jeep and set to work. The boys helped their mom do the dishes and put everything away. The boys came over to watch Dan install the locks. Mason had a million questions about how Dan was doing things. Dan patiently answered every question. The sun was dipping behind the trees as he put the tool bag back in the jeep and announced that his job was done.

Elizabeth and the boys trailed Dan Flatt to his jeep, and he turned around and thanked her for supper and knelt down and gave each boy a firm handshake. "Glad to meet you boys," he said, "I hope we can all get together again sometime soon." He stood up and met her eyes as she said, "Go back inside boys, Mr. Flatt and I need to discuss something in private."

"Mom!" they wailed, "Can't we listen too?" "Shoo, get going!" They both shrugged and went back inside. "Betcha a dollar they're watching us right now," said Dan. "Oh, I'm sure of that," said Elizabeth. She stepped closer and gave him a light kiss on the lips. There came a squeal of laughter from the house. "Thanks again for saving me, Mister Dan Flatt." And for coming back into my life, she thought. He turned her around and they moved on to the porch and sat down on the swing, where they had spent many summer nights together, talking, kissing, holding each other, and watching the stars. Dan gave the swing a little shove so they could rock slowly. The same stars were watching over them again tonight, just as they had years ago. Dan thought some things never change. Now look where we are, after all these years. He smiled inwardly, and held her a little closer. Dan said, "You know, it seems like we've just been transported back in time about 15 years."

The evening breeze was just enough to keep the bugs away. In the darkness, it seemed like the whole world had shrunk down to just the two of them.

"You know, you used to be my best friend in the whole world," said Elizabeth. "Then you went away to college. We just drifted apart, I guess. I got so lonely, found another guy, thought he was as good as you, since it seemed like you weren't coming back, we got married, had two kids, got divorced, and now look at us. I mean you and me. It almost seems like there was a time warp or something and we're still together just like it used to be, except for those two little rug rats."

He gently laid her head against his shoulder. She used to do that when they were dating, and he loved the feel of her against him. "It does feel good," he said.

She sat up and turned to face him. Her eyes were moist. "I'm not sure I should even ask this, but do you think we could pick up where we left off, all those years ago, or should we even consider it?"

Dan put his arm around her and said, "I don't just think we should consider it, I think we should DO it." Her moist eyes filled with tears as he pulled her to him and kissed her. A little while later, they relaxed some, she had her head in his lap, her feet hanging out over the end of the porch swing. "It's been a long time since I've been this happy."

"Me too."

A noise from the window made them look, only to find two sets of elbows side by side, framing the window.

"How long have you guys been there?" Elizabeth asked sternly.

"Well," said Mikey," You guys really got mushy there. We figured we should make sure you didn't get carried away or anything."

Elizabeth jumped off the swing and lunged at the window, laughing, "I'm going to get you two and carry YOU away!" The boys screamed in laughter and raced for their bedroom.

When she came back, she sat down on the porch swing and said "Well, we're going to have to watch what we're doing when we're around those two." They laughed. "But I have something I want to talk to you about. Seriously." Dan reached out to pull her to him, but she stayed put and said "Really, seriously. We need to talk. About this money I found."

"Ok. I guess party time's over." Dan shrugged and sat up.

"You know I found a bunch of money a couple of days ago. Did I tell you how much I counted?" He shook his head.

"I counted two hundred thousand dollars in that old knapsack that was in the trunk." Dan let out a low whistle. "It was in your basement, right? All these years?"

"Yes." Elizabeth told him about the talk she had with her grandmother. It was her grandmother who had hidden the knapsack full of money in the trunk.

"Where's the money now? She looked at him a little sheepishly. "It's in the trunk of my car."

"What!"

"Well, I didn't know what to do with it. I can't just take it to the bank and say 'Oh, I want to deposit this money in my checking or savings account.' Those people at the bank would go nuts at the sight of all that money. Then, they'd probably call the FBI who would think I was a drug dealer or something and confiscate the money and probably arrest me. So you see what a problem I have?" She looked defeated. "What should I do?"

"I think you should rent a large safety deposit box. If you can't get a large enough one, then rent another one at another bank somewhere. That money needs to be kept safe, until you can figure out what to do with it. In fact, I think I would check around and fine someplace that deals in old money, probably in St Louis, and take several bills and see if they're worth more than face value. You could sell them some, but I had a friend once who bought and sold old money like this on e-bay. Takes a lot longer but you could maybe double your investment. Sound like a plan?"

Elizabeth looked at him and said, "I had already thought of part of that, but I wanted a second opinion. I'll do that tomorrow. Thank you." She kissed him, then pulled away. "But that's not what I wanted to talk to you about."

"Now what?"

She recounted what Howard Bailey had told her about the coal mines being out of business, and that she should just keep the money. "My great grandfather just disappeared when all this happened. It really broke up my great grandmother as well my grandmother." She sat upright on the swing and turned to face him. She took both his hands in hers and said, "I want to know what happened to him. Where ever he is the train will probably be there, too. I don't think the authorities tried very hard to find him or the train. Coal Companies weren't very highly thought of back then. Same thing with Wells Fargo. But, it would mean a great deal to my grandmother and to me, too. When you have time, will you help me find out what happened to him? Please, Please?"

A small voice from the window said, "it'll be just like a TV show!" Another voice said "Yeah! A real mystery! Right here!"

Dan looked long and hard at her and said, "Sure. I'll do it. No, we ALL should do this together. He was looking at the boys when he said it. He could see the excited look on their faces. Then he looked back at Elizabeth and said, "They made me do it, ya know."

Elizabeth jumped up from the swing and said, "You guys are in trouble now!" and ran for the door. Two little voices squealed as they raced for the safety of their bedrooms. At the door, she turned back to Dan and said softly, "Thank you. So much." She held out her hand. He took it, pulled her close to him and put his arms around her. She smelled like fresh soap. One long kiss led to another.

Sometime later, Dan went home.

*   *   *   *   *   *   *

The next evening, the four of them sat around on the living room floor and brainstormed about how someone would go about finding a lost train: a real live lost train, not a toy. A huge bowl of popcorn sat in the middle. Elizabeth said "Oh, by the way, I rented a safety deposit box during my lunch hour. I got the biggest one they offered." She looked at the boys, then at Dan. "The, er, stuff just barely fit." The boys hadn't noticed anything.

Dan unpacked his laptop and googled 'old train graveyards'. They spent an hour searching for placed an old train might have been parked after its useful life was over. The nearest place was French Lick, Indiana. Dan called up Google Earth and looked at an aerial view of French Lick and they decided that it was worth a drive there to check it out, and let the boys see a real old train. Then the boys came up with missing persons, which didn't exist back then; and Mikey said

"Why wouldn't the sheriff know all about stuff like that", and every body turned to him in awe. "Well, that's what they do on TV."

"Mikey, that's a great answer," said Elizabeth. She turned to Dan. "Well, would they know or have records from back then still today, somewhere?"

Dan thought about it. "Probably. But I don't know where. I'll check around tomorrow."

"Elizabeth said, Dan, tomorrow is a school holiday. So, I'm taking the day off from work to be with the boys. Maybe we could all go with you, huh?"

"Yeah, Dan! Let's all go!" the boys screamed. That night, lying in bed at his mother's house, he stared at the blackness of the ceiling, hands behind his head, thinking about how excited the boys were. That gave him a warm feeling he hadn't known before. It really didn't worry him. It was just...different. Like he wasn't sure about this feeling, but didn't want it to go away. He finally drifted off.

The next morning, his mother hovered over him, serving biscuits and gravy and hot rolls fresh from the old oven. She finally sat down with her coffee.

"Mom, I've got a question for you," said Dan. Staring at her intently.

"Well, I've got an answer for you," she said. "Marry that woman, quick before she gets away again."

Dan was so surprised he spilled coffee down his shirt, then stood up abruptly and knocked his plate onto the floor. His mother looked like she's seen a ghost. She jumped up almost as quickly, and scooped the plate from the floor. He dabbed at his shirt with his napkin. Then Dan started laughing. He laughed and laughed then his mother joined in and they both sat down again at the table, tears in their eyes. "Wow, mom, you really threw me there."

"Well, I have been watching you for the last couple of weeks and every time you come back from her place you look really happy. The last few years, when you were here, you were all business but this time, business seems to be taking a back seat, because you spend a lot of time over at her place. Even though you supposedly came here to fix MY place. She smiled. "That was a little dig."

I've been doing some thinking about her and her boys. There's something I can't put my finger on, but I think I'm going to have to do something about it. You approve?"

"Oh my, yes. I do. I'd love to have her for a daughter in law." She put down her coffee cup.

"You want me to call her and give her the good news?"

"Mom!" he shrieked.

"Well, I knew something was on your mind this morning when you came down to breakfast." "Guess what Mom, that wasn't even close to what I wanted to ask you."

His mother poured them each another cup of coffee. "Well?" she waited. Dan said, "We have decided to look into finding this train her great grandfather was on when he disappeared. I know it's probably a wild goose chase. You're pretty smart. You have any idea where we could look? Since the train was stolen, or robbed then stolen, would the sheriff's office have records that go back that far?"

"I doubt it. But the Historical Society might. They're in the old house the jail was in at the turn of the century. Behind city hall. You could ask there."

Dan said, "We were brainstorming last night, and that's one place we never thought of. Thanks mom."

Dan called Elizabeth and they decided to take the boys with them and show them what history looked like. The huge old stone building with a wide front porch sat just off the square in downtown Marion. At one time, the sheriff's office was often the focal point of many arrests and even some hangings on the side of the building. The gallows were gone, but inside the office, lining the walls were photos of unlucky (mostly) men who ended their earthly journey while being watched by sometimes hundreds of onlookers who cheered and jeered as they strangled on their last breath.

Today, the old jail was strangely quiet outside. Inside, two very elderly women and one frail old man were sorting and typing and filing. They all looked up as the four newcomers walked in. "Help you folks?" said one old woman.

"Yes" said Elizabeth. "We're looking for some information concerning a train robbery in the 1920's. The train was robbed, then stolen and never found." "Oh dear," said the old woman, "I don't think ever heard of a train being stolen around here. Have you Evelyn?"

The other woman, Evelyn, said "Well yes, I have, but only a little bit. Georgina, you don't even remember your birthday, much less any history." That brought a chuckle from the old man. Georgina said, "Shut up Gerald. Or you can fix your own supper."

Evelyn paused, cleared her throat and said, "Are you members of the historical society?" Elizabeth said, "Uh,no. Do we need to be?" Evelyn said, "Well, for just $20 per year, we'll give you all the help we can. But without the money to help us stay open, I'm afraid you're on your own." Dan slipped a $20 bill from his wallet and handed it to the old lady, who made it disappear like magic. She produced an information card and a pen. "Fill this out and you're all set."

A few moments later, she led them up a flight of stairs to another room filled with journals. Mason said "Smells like dust in here." Then he sneezed. It didn't seem to bother the old woman as she peered intently at a row of green bindings.

She hefted one from its place and handed it to Dan. It was heavy, each binding the size of a full newspaper page. "Each one of these binders holds a month of the Marion Daily newspapers. "See where they're dated on the side. Do you know when the train was robbed?" "Not exactly. I think it was 1927."

We've been slowly putting these old newspapers onto microfiche. But, the technology has changed again and fiche readers are now like carrier pigeons. Out of date. Sort of like the three of us who run this place. Now they want us to scan everything and put it on computer. I admit it's easier, but now it seems like we have to start all over again." She sighed, then sat down in an old wooden telegrapher's chair. "It just never ends." "Do you have a scanner big enough to scan a newspaper page?" asked Dan.

"No," she said. "We don't have much of a budget, and a scanner like that costs about five hundred dollars. We simply can't afford it right now. We do have a new computer if we ever get a scanner like that. The computer will do the job."

Elizabeth and the boys began with January 1927 and turned each page of the newspaper until they reached August, when Mason pointed to a photo of a train and said "There, Mom!" On the front page was a story about the train being robbed, then stolen. The story went on to tell how the miners were threatening a strike if they didn't get paid on time. The police had no clue as to the whereabouts of the train and few people had seen anything that would help. Speculators said the Birger and Shelton gangs were at it again, but representatives from both outlaw gangs denied any involvement in this one caper. The poor conductor's body was found along the tracks and taken to a local funeral home where it was put on display until the funeral. Accounts differed from police to railroad officials to Consolidated Coal officers as to the amount of money stolen. Wells Fargo was on the hook for insuring the money and they promptly paid up to avert any problems at the mine. Wells Fargo itself was initiating a search for its missing agent along with the money. The very next day, the story about the train robbery was delegated to second page because Charles Lindbergh had successfully crossed the Atlantic. Also sharing front-page space was the news about the disastrous fire at the Ozark Hotel in Creal Springs.

Dan read the accounts twice then read further. The story fizzled out after a couple of days, with no mention of it after three days. Other news took its place. It seems even the local police departments had not investigated any further.

Dan found daily Police reports from the Herrin City Police Department tucked into a corner of the main 'library' room. Judging from the size of the Herrin journals compared to Marion police reports, Marion was a quiet city. From the dates of the robbery, the police had not seemed to try very hard to solve the case. The detective assigned to the case made few notes and did not follow up on many leads. Possibly because 1927 was a very busy year for the police and an unstable year for coal mines and unions around Herrin, with shootings and lynchings nearly every week. So a mere train robbery was put on the back burner? One newspaper account from the Marion Daily said an elderly woman was awakened from her sound sleep around two am by her little dog Buster, who insisted he be let out of the house so he could relieve himself. While standing in the doorway waiting for the dog to return, a train passed thru town, completely dark, and showing no lights that she could see. She thought it odd with no lights, but soon went back to sleep. It was only when she mentioned it to her neighbor that she decided to file a police report. The police evidently thought nothing of it.

The boys soon tired of looking at old historical things and Elizabeth announced that they should all go home. Dan dropped them off then proceeded to his mother's house, where he spent the afternoon scraping paint. He decided that when all the paint had been scraped off, the house would probably fall down without the paint holding it all together.

Chapter Six

Dan Flatt spent the morning on a ladder painting parts of the second story of his mom's house. It was something he had done twice before, over a span of more than a few years, but it seemed to get harder each time he had to go up and down the aluminum ladder and reposition it. He had tried to talk his mom into having vinyl siding installed on the house but she insisted that paint looked better. Besides, she had free labor in the form of her only son to do the work.

He climbed down the ladder for the umpteenth time this morning and decided that he would take the rest of the day off. He put the ladder away, and put the lid back on the paint and cleaned the brushes. With everything stored away, he stopped in his mom's kitchen, where she made him a thick ham and cheese sandwich and a tall glass of iced tea, which tasted great, considering how hot the temperatures were today.

His mom was putting away some plates. She closed the cabinet door and turned to Dan. "I think it's great that you and Elizabeth are back together again, but it's been a few years and some things have changed. You realize that?

Dan said, "Seems like just yesterday we were dating, mom. I agree that we're more mature than we were back then, but I plan to pick up where I left off, where she's concerned."

"You know she has those two boys," said his mother. "What do you think about that? Do they make a difference?

"They like me, and I like them, too. I think we get along pretty well. But, I've only seen them a couple of times. You know, they could be little monsters. You know, terrorizing the neighborhood after dark, scaring the neighbor's dogs and cats, and stuff."

His mother laughed. "If I know Elizabeth, and believe me I think I do, those boys are as well behaved as any kids you'll find anywhere. That poor girl has had a tough time of it. For a while after you two went your separate ways, it seemed like things would turn out just fine for her. After she graduated from college and nurses school, she met a guy who had just moved to town and took a job as superintendent at the high school. They got married and had the two boys and moved into a nice house out on the west side to town in that new subdivision. Then, I guess things started happening between them. And one night, the police discovered him and his secretary stark naked in the backseat of their car, out in the cemetery. After that, there were two divorces and everybody left town, except for Elizabeth. She stayed here, much to her credit, and moved into her grandmother's house with her boys. A couple of years ago, her grandmother went to the nursing home and now Elizabeth has that big old house just for herself and her boys." She patted Dan's hand. "I'm glad you two are back together again."

He got in the jeep and headed toward the pasture where he used to fly his ultralight airplane. The big old barn at the far end of the field was where he stored his little craft.

The doors opened easily, since he had periodically kept them greased. When opened, the sunlight penetrated the darkness, revealing a purple and yellow contraption that Dan Flatt likened to 'a couple of lawn chairs under a wing with a motor in the back'. He pulled off a clear plastic drop cloth that was covering the plane to keep birds from building nests, and was pleased at how clean the plane still was.

He spent the afternoon tearing down and then rebuilding the engine. He added fresh gas from a can in the backseat of the jeep, and installed a new battery behind the seats. Then he pulled the plane out into the sunlight in front of the barn. After pulling the prop thru a few times by hand, he sat down in the pilot's seat and flipped the switch to on, then pressed the starter button. The prop whirled around several times, then caught and fired up with a wonderful sounding roar that only a two stroke engine can make. He ran the engine a few minutes then shut it off. Then, he began a thorough inspection of the entire airplane, to make sure every nut and bolt was where it should be and tight. Then, he inspected the fabric for rips and soft spots and found everything to be just as he had left it.

He strapped himself into the pilot's seat, and put on a pair of shooting muffs to keep the noise down to a manageable roar, and fired up the engine. Next came a pair of clear goggles. He put his feet on the rudder pedals and moved his hand to the throttle next to the seat. With a look around him to make sure he wasn't about to get in the way of a stray deer or whatever, he moved the throttle to full and the little airplane bounced over the grass and quickly picked up speed. Dan Flatt eased the control stick back towards his lap and the plane jumped into the air, eager to be free from the confines of the earth.

As he gained some altitude, and swept over the trees south of his airfield, he marveled at how much he really enjoyed flying. Even though he flew for a living, and flew all kinds of airplanes from small Cessnas and Pipers to Boeings and other big jets, this little ultralight embodied the true meaning of flight to him. This was flying at it's simplest, about what the Wright Bothers would have felt like over a hundred years ago, with the wind singing thru the wires. He angled the airplane away from the town and headed towards some areas he had enjoyed flying over before. Fields where he could actually zoom down and chase deer. The deer were fast but he was faster, and he had actually touched his nose wheel to the back of a young buck once as it tried to race away from him one summer evening. From an altitude of just five hundred feet, he could see about five miles in any direction. He flew aimlessly, enjoying the wind in his face. He let his mind wander, and then he thought about Elizabeth some, and her boys, and something about being around them made him feel....good. After a while, he realized he had been daydreaming and not paying attention to his flying.

He was disoriented. He flew on for a while and a small village showed up ahead. He swooped down towards the middle of town, and read the name painted on the side of the water tower. The name said Simpson. Aha! He had been flying in a huge circle, and hadn't been paying attention. This was a bare bones flying machine, no GPS, no radio, only a compass and altimeter. Now he knew where he was. He turned the plane around in a gentle bank and flew towards home.

Chapter Seven

Dan Flatt drove back to his mother's. His mother was watching TV in the kitchen when he came thru the back door. "You should be in the family room, Mom," he said, "It's probably a lot more comfortable in the recliner than it is in here."

"I like it here," she said, "besides I can prop my chin up with my elbows if my head gets too heavy."

"Then you should be going to bed," Dan said.

"I have never gotten used to having a TV in my bedroom. That's where I sleep, not watch TV. I know some people do, but I don't like it."

"Ok, Ok," said Dan Flatt. His cell phone chimed. It was a text message telling him to check his e-mail.

"Who was that?" said his mom. "More work, probably," Dan studied the caller ID then put his phone away.

In his room, he took his laptop from its case and brought it to life, and went out onto the internet. His e-mail came up and he found the file he was looking for. He read it thru, then he forwarded it to his partner CJ. He and CJ worked as a team recovering aircraft for banks from around the United States. Dan usually did the flying, and held licenses and ratings for many different kinds of airplanes, where CJ took care of fixing things like engines that wouldn't start, or picking locks on the doors of jets. However, in a pinch CJ could fly almost as many types of airplanes as Dan. The company he and CJ worked for sent them on 'missions' that had them retrieving Cessnas and Pipers, Beechcraft and Mooney airplanes as well as small business jets. In today's economy, a small business jet could sell for anywhere from five to fifty million dollars new, and half that used. So, banks were not eager to write off a loan for that kind of money. And if the person or company who bought the airplane decided not to make their loan payments or give the plane back, Dan and CJ were sometimes called to get the airplane back however they could, without hurting anybody. Even then, some areas of the United States where they needed to bring an airplane back from, the authorities were not always friendly to repo men. So, a clandestine approach was sometimes necessary. CJ and Dan had worked as a team for several years, and had an impressive recovery record. Their recovery exploits had sometimes been pretty dramatic, almost the stuff of James Bond novels.

Whereas Dan Flatt had grown up in a small town in southern Illinois, and preferred the rural life, CJ had grown up in Los Angeles, a product of a Cuban neighborhoods. He lived for fast cars, bright lights and a new date every night. Dan sent CJ a text informing him of the forwarded e-mail. He received a phone call a minute later.

"Danny boy, I was just saying to myself that it's been awhile since I had heard from you and it was about time, and lo and behold! My phone gives me a text message. What gives?"

"Read your e-mail and then send me your thoughts by return e-mail. Then we'll work from there. Adios my friend." "Ok, then. Tomorrow you will hear from me. Tonight, I have friends to entertain. See ya, Gringo!"

Even though California was two time zones earlier than Illinois, Dan Flatt received a call from his friend at ten o'clock the next morning. He put the paint scraper down on the porch step where he had started two hours earlier. "This is early for you, CJ."

"Well, my evening didn't progress as I thought it would." The little Cuban sounded resigned. "Sometimes those things happen, you know. So, I had plenty of time to read up on this next, er, project of ours. Have you got a plan?"

Dan Flatt said, "Well, I do, but like all plans of ours, we need to talk this thing over, and also, we need to do some more research. The plane is currently residing at a small towered airport at Kinston, North Carolina. I did a little b'essing with the maintenance director at the FBO there by phone. I told him I had a friend who had a jet nearby and I was thinking about getting some maintenance done on my plane. I think he was trying to drum up more business for the FBO, so I kept him going awhile. He said the plane was there for routine maintenance checks but he also said they were planning to repaint the plane in a week or so, as soon as a slot came up in the paint shop on the field. CJ said, "Hmmm. Something tells me that maybe the plane will get a new N number as well as a shiny new paint job. Then with a new N number and a different paint job the plane would theoretically 'disappear'."

"Yeah, I thought about that, too."

They agreed to meet right away, with CJ flying into Marion the next day. Then they would come up with a plan to retrieve the plane.

That evening, while sitting on Elizabeth's front porch swing after a wonderful meal of fried chicken and all the trimmings, Dan Flatt explained to her that he would be out of town for several days and when he returned, they would start work on finding their 'treasure'. Elizabeth said, "I never asked before, but what sort of work do you do, Dan?"

"I work for a company that works with banks and finance companies here in the U.S.," Dan said. "I am what you might call a 'reposition' specialist." She looked at him slowly and said, "Oh." Dan could tell she was confused by his title. "So, you move things around?"

"Well, sort of." He smiled, but wasn't any more forthcoming. Just then, the boys came thru the front door and plopped down in front of the swing. "When are we gonna go look for the train, Dan?"

"Soon, guys. In a few days. I have to leave tomorrow," he said. Mikey said, "Where ya goin' Dan?" Dan replied, "I have to help a friend do some moving. It won't take long, and before you know it, it will be the weekend and we'll be about ready to go search for that treasure, as you guys call it." They jumped up and ran back inside. Mikey hollered thru the screen door, "You can kiss her now; we won't watch." They laughed and Dan Flatt did just that.

Later that night, he got on the internet at his mom's house and again started searching for places that had abandoned train cars. He was surprised that there were so many places that railroads had simply left locomotives and other old rail cars. He counted six places where old locomotives were supposed to be and located them on his road atlas. That would make for interesting road trips for Elizabeth and especially the boys.

The next morning, they all piled into Dan's Jeep and drove down to Grand Tower, IL., along the Mississippi River. After asking directions at the local Quik Stop store, they found a small locomotive nearly hidden by bushes and trees that had grown up around the old engine and coal car. The old locomotive showed years and years of rust and disuse. The boys screamed with delight as they descended upon the train cars. Dan helped the boys into the cab and they took turns playing engineer and blowing an imaginary whistle. Dan and Elizabeth examined the locomotive and took photos of it. Then they all piled back into the Jeep and went in search of someone who would know about the history behind the train. They found what they were looking for. His name was Abner, and he appeared to be about as ancient as the old engine itself. Abner told them that he had been the fireman on that engine since it was bought new in 1948. It had been purchased by the old electric company before Ameren bought them out. They would make runs to Joppa, Illinois and pick up coal and return to the power plant in Grand Tower. He also said that if they would look on the fireman's (left) side of the engine, just in front of the cab, they would see a two foot diameter hole where the little engine had given up life, back in 1961. The boiler had exploded, and Abner and the engineer both had been burned by flying pieces of steel plate from the boiler. After that, the engine had been mothballed and the power company had coal delivered by truck. Dan asked him if he knew about the train that had vanished back in 1926. Abner said that was before he was born, and besides, he hadn't heard of anything like that, and he knew most of the train folks around Southern Illinois. He wasn't aware of any other engines hiding around this part of the state, either. They thanked him and left.

On the way back home, they discussed a future road trip to Indiana to look at the train cars Dan had found on Google Earth. The boys were looking forward to the trip. Dan and Elizabeth just looked at each other and smiled.

Dan told them that he had to work out of town for a few days, and that he would be leaving in the next day or two. When he got back, they would plan their next trip in detail.

Chapter Eight

The East Coast night sky was completely covered with a thick layer of clouds. There was no moon or stars tonight. Three o'clock in the morning around the executive airport in Southern New Jersey and the stillness was complete. Even the security guard whose job it was to patrol the airport grounds was dozing in his car between the back of a large hangar and a parked snowplow. His alarm clock was set to rouse him every 45 minutes for his hourly tour of the perimeter. Some nights, he just reset the clock and dozed for another hour. Nothing ever happened on his shift.

Two days before, Dan Flatt and CJ Rodriguez had flown into North Carolina in a rented Cessna, along with a hired jump plane pilot from Southern Illinois they had used before. His name was Larry. He was an older man, tall and lean, but willing to try almost anything, even if just for the thrill of doing it, other than the money. He almost always had a grin on his face. His favorite phrase was "Yeeha!"

They had spent part of a day wandering around the airport, posing as prospective maintenance customers, so they could check out the airport, and determine what security was in place and how hard it would be to steal the jet they were after. By early afternoon, they had their recon complete. They retired to the hotel they were staying at a dozen miles away, near another small airport where their Cessna was parked. Dan, CJ and Larry each had a room. Dan could hear the little Cuban thru the wall, snoring like a buzzsaw. As sleep began to settle over him, his thoughts turned back to Elizabeth and the boys and their search for 'treasure'. If nothing else, they would all have a good time together. He finally drifted off and what seemed like five minutes later his alarm went off. Time to go to work, even if it was the middle of the night. The three of them quietly gathered up their gear, left the motel and drove to the little airport. The airport was eerily quiet in the middle of the night darkness, as they untied their plane. Because of security and a well fenced perimeter, they couldn't just drive into the airport and steal the plane. They would have to be a lot more discreet. They would fly over the Kinston airport at six thousand feet, enough time to jump away from the Cessna and steer their chutes down thru the clouds and onto the airport grounds. At six thousand feet of altitude, the Cessna could not be heard from the ground. By the time their GPS centered on the airport below, Dan Flatt had positioned himself on the strut of the plane, with CJ ready to jump right behind him. Larry cut the engine and let the airspeed fall away to a mere seventy miles per hour. "See ya later Larry!" yelled Dan over the noise of the engine and the rushing air past the open door. Dan Flatt let go of the wingstrut and dropped backwards into the black void below, and disappeared into the night. A few seconds later, CJ went, too. Larry slammed the door shut, and yelled "Yeehah!" and goosed the throttle back to normal cruise. He would orbit the area in case something went haywire, and he had to make an emergency pickup. He had done that before, for these guys. Not everything was a piece of cake. Down thru the night air they fell, at one hundred twenty five miles per hour towards certain death, if the chute didn't open. They entered the clouds and almost as quickly fell out the bottom of the overcast and the airport was right below them, as planned. A strong yank on the ripcord, and Dan was jerked upright and slowed instantly. The ground raced up to meet him as he bent his knees for the jolt of impact with the ground. He'd done many "standing" landings and this time was no different.

On the ground, Dan Flatt gathered the chute in his arms and listened for any signs of activity. CJ had landed gently on the tarmac fifty feet away and did the same, standing still as a statue and listening for any tell tale signs that they had been discovered. They heard nothing.

No airplanes were moving at that time of night, and this airport had no scheduled airline service, just the occasional charter flight and those almost never happened in the dead of night. So the airport slept on soundly, and was deserted save for the lone security guard. No one noticed the two black clad skydivers descend out of the inky darkness of the sky and touch down softly on the tarmac. After gathering up their chutes, they made their way to a Business jet tied down on the ramp between several other jets. This jet was not the largest, nor was it the smallest on the ramp, but it was their target tonight.

Dan Flatt took a key from his pocket and opened the airstair door. He stood aside as it hissed down to the ground. He then quietly darted up the stairs and entered the cockpit. The second man scurried across the ramp towards a small building that housed three tugs, used to tow planes around. He sprayed the door to the building with lithium grease to make sure the hinges did not squeal when opened. These tugs used propane gas engines and therefore made less noise than a gas or diesel engine, more like the hum a forklift made. He selected a tug from the building and headed towards the jet. Then he positioned the tug in front of the jet and hitched the towbar to the front wheels. He then removed the wheel chocks holding the plane in place at the tiedown area. In the cockpit, Dan Flatt opened the pilot's side window and leaned out, giving CJ a thumbs up sign to indicate the brakes were off. The tug began to slowly back up, moving the jet across the ramp.

The big jet followed the tug down the down the taxiway, like an elephant would follow a man with its leash, over a mile to the far end of the airport, where they were not likely to be heard when they started up the powerful jet engines. Once at the far end, CJ unhooked the tug from the front wheels and drove it into the weeds beside the taxiway. He then ascended the airstair door into the airplane and closed it behind him. He climbed into the co-pilot's seat and adjusted the seat to fit properly and began reading the 'before takeoff' checklist out loud to Dan.

The guard roused himself from his sleep and adjusted his body behind the wheel. He had to go to the bathroom. It was just more than just having to take a whizz against the snowplow, so this called for a trip to the FBO office. Oh well, he thought, another few minutes and the damn alarm would have gone off anyway. Might as well get this round done with after I hit the bathroom. He started the car and drove from around the hangar across the ramp to the FBO office. He paid no attention to the row of planes parked there, as he unlocked the office and hurried inside to take care of his pressing problem. A few minutes later, he left the office, relocked the building and got back in his car. His rounds called for him to start at the end hangar, make sure the walk-in "people" doors were locked and note the time. He slowly drove down the row of planes towards the end hangar. Something was nagging at him. Something just didn't seem to be right. So, he turned around and drove slowly down the row of planes again. What was it?

Then it dawned on him that earlier in the evening, there had been five planes in the back row of jets and now there were only four. Was there a departure? A departure should have been on his schedule, because he for damn sure wouldn't be caught sleeping when there were people around. He hadn't heard anything, and he was sure he would have heard a jet, for god's sakes. What was going on? Was he losing it? He got out of the car and walked around where the jet had been parked, as if the ground could give him a clue as to the whereabouts of the jet. He was about to climb back into his car when he heard a jet's engines come alive for takeoff. Suddenly the runway lights snapped on. The guard knew that could be done by several clicks of a microphone on the tower frequency. He could tell the plane was racing down the runway because the whine of the jet engines was getting louder. He could barely see the big business jet in the darkness as it passed low overhead, showing no landing lights or even running lights on. In seconds the airplane was swallowed up by the clouds. The sound faded almost as quickly. Had he really seen what he just saw? It never occurred to him that an airplane, and a very expensive airplane at that, had just been stolen right from under his sleeping nose.

Dan Flatt looked at CJ and they high fived each other. Dan just grinned. As they popped out on top of the clouds, they were treated to a moonless night. Because the clouds kept the city lights out like a blanket,

the night sky was a surreal setting with the twinkling lights from mil-
lions of stars. The airspeed read nearly five hundred miles per hour,
and Dan Flatt stretched his lean, six foot body as much as he could
within the confines of the pilot's seat, and ran a hand thru his dark,
wavy hair. CJ, on the other hand was just the opposite. He was a short
plump little Cuban, who was not only a pilot but one of those people
who loved to break things just so he could fix them, and was a master
mechanic. Bathed in the greenish glow of instrument lights, he pulled
out a Cuban cigar and ran the length of it beneath his nose and sighed,
then put it back in his shirt pocket. He couldn't smoke it in here. It
wouldn't do to have this nice beautiful multi-million dollar jet with its
fine leather, teak and mahogany panels and accents clogged with cigar
smoke before they gave it back to the bank. They stayed below three
thousand feet so the radar wouldn't pick them up and, instead of setting the autopilot, Dan decided to hand fly the nimble jet back towards
the Midwest. They had one stop to make, at a small airport at Lima,
Ohio to take on fuel, then they would lift off one last time and set the
autopilot to head for an executive airport outside of Chicago and hand
over the keys to a grateful bank. Some very big companies, not to
mention some very well known famous names around the US of A oc-
casionally defaulted on their loans to banks that liked to cater to the
rich, fast and famous. And when these rich, fast and famous types became indignant at handing over their toys when they couldn't pay,
banks hired people like Dan Flatt and his partner CJ to retrieve the
bank's property. Most handed over the keys without any fuss, but
some would go to great lengths to hide their airplanes so they couldn't
be found. Which made their job a little more creative. As long as these
folks hadn't bought off the law, which sometimes had happened in the
past, the job wasn't too dangerous. After ten years of working together, Dan and CJ had only a few close calls. They'd been shot at several
times, and even jailed once when a small town sheriff changed the law
to fit his rich friends' needs. Another time they'd made off with another small jet only to have engine trouble and make an emergency
landing in a swamp in Georgia. That plane was still there, submerged
in fifteen feet of brackish snake and alligator infested water. And once

when trying to take off from a river in Minnesota, their float equipped plane had run into a submerged log in the darkness and flipped over. Today however, was a piece of cake. Another repo job completed, then home to bed.

Tomorrow, with no other repo jobs scheduled, CJ was booked on a flight to Miami to see his mom and her side of the family at a traditional Cuban family reunion, only on American soil. And Dan Flatt was headed back to Southern Illinois in his Jeep to see his mom and continue doing much needed repairs on her old house in Carterville. Or was it because he really wanted to get back to see Elizabeth? The chance meeting in the grocery store had sent his heart fluttering, more so than it ever had when they were dating back in high school. Was it because she was a mature beautiful woman? Or was it because she had two young boys? Or had the thought of settling down entered his mind, a thought that he'd never had before?

The small jet touched down in the early morning hours at a suburban Chicago airport, and taxied to a large modern FBO called, appropriately, 'Million Aire' Services. The staff there had handled many "returns" for the bank over the years and were prepared to hide the airplane from searching eyes if necessary until all the bank's paperwork would be processed with the FAA.

Dan and CJ accepted a ride in the courtesy van to O'Hare Airport, where they parted company. CJ boarded an American Airlines flight to Miami, and Dan headed for the commuter airline that would eventually set him down in Marion, Illinois, the closest airline he could fly to Carterville. He would be home by eight O'clock p.m., then up tomorrow and ready to tackle his mom's house.

Chapter Nine

The next day, Junior was back at work, after having posted bail, which consisted of the title and the keys to his truck, since he had no money otherwise. The card players watched him as he finished his shift, then left, on foot. That evening Junior sat at an outside table at the Dairy Queen licking an ice cream cone. Peanut drove up and parked and went inside. He came out with a large chocolate covered cone and sat down beside Junior.

"You sure have some dumbass luck, my man," said Peanut, wiping his hands on his jeans.

Junior nodded glumly. "At least before, I had my old truck. Now I don't even have that. And I am NOT going to ride a bicycle around town. I need to get some money to pay back that damn bail bonds guy. Pretty soon he's gonna want it all paid in full. They don't give you but so much credit, ya know."

Peanut said, "I been thinking about another line of work. Something we could do in our spare time apart from our regular jobs that might just bring us in some quick cash." He licked all the way around his cone. "You interested?"

"Hell yeah. Tell me more."

Peanut looked around them, then lowered his voice some. "My cousin out in Pennsylvania has been doing this for some time. He rides around with a couple of other guys at night out in the suburbs and if they see a four wheeler or garden tractor or dirt bike or something like that, if they can, they grab 'em. They then turn 'em over to a guy who will pay quick cash for that stuff and the merchandise is never seen again. I think that stuff winds up down in Mississippi or Alabama someplace like that, where country folks get what they want for a good price and don't ask too many questions. If you know what I mean?"

"Damn," said Junior. "This sound pretty easy. They ever get caught?" "Not yet." "How much has your cousin made?" Peanut smiled. "He told me one week they made almost three thousand dollars. But that was a pretty big haul. Most nights he tells me they get about three to five hundred each. But that's better wages than you're making, working in a nursing home, cleaning up shit."

"Damn straight," said Junior. He was suddenly feeling better about his future. "We ought to look around a little and see if the pickin's are good around here. What do you think?"

Peanut said, "I think we should finish our ice cream cones and take a drive."

Chapter Ten

Howard Bailey read the article about the break-in at Elizabeth Jennings' home thru twice. He thought about their previous meeting there in the great room at the nursing home, and the young orderly who was busy polishing everything in sight while they talked about the money she found. Howard decided the orderly must be gifted with exceptionally good hearing, if he picked up everything they said and was able to find her home after work. He figured the orderly must have followed Elizabeth home in order to find her house. It was just dumb luck that Sam Henderson saw the orderly get out of his truck and call the police. He had seen the orderly back at work today but the young man was keeping a low profile. Somebody else was dusting furniture in the great room. Howard had a feeling that the orderly was probably doomed to be changing bedpans in another wing of the nursing home for some time.

He was pleasantly surprised to see Elizabeth the next day. She smiled at him as she crossed the great room, while looking around her, probably for the orderly.

"That young man still works here, but he's on bedpan duty, or something like that, probably forever," said Howard Bailey. They shared a laugh about that. He patted her hand. "This is like a real life whodunnit; more fun that I've had in ages. What brings you back here so soon?" She started to speak, then abruptly stopped as a tall, well dressed older gentleman with styled silver hair pulled up a chair next to them and stuck out his hand at Elizabeth. "Howard always tries to keep the good looking girls to himself, so I'm not waiting for an introduction. My name is Stuart Woods. I live just down the Hall from this old coot." He indicated Howard Bailey. "I hear you got your house broke into?" he said.

"Yes," said Elizabeth, "But they didn't get anything that I can see. It's a mystery, why anyone would want to pick on me." She looked at Howard, who was mum. Howard said to Stuart, "Elizabeth is trying to figure out what happened to her great-grandfather; he was the Wells Fargo agent that was on the coal mine payroll train that disappeared back in the 1920's. It's never been found. You remember anything about that Stuart?"

Stuart Woods snorted, "Howard, I'm not THAT old!" He stroked his chin. "I suppose it could have been hidden in an old mine shaft or a tunnel somewhere. I imagine a whole bunch of folks probably checked that aspect out, don't you?" What about an old tunnel a train could hide in? Something like that?" Stuart shook his head. "I'm not aware of any tunnels around here that a train could hide in," he said.

Howard Bailey said, "The only tunnel I know of is the Tunnel Hill trail tunnel, and people ride their bicycles thru that one every day, so I don't think there's a train hidden there. I don't know anybody who's still alive who lives down that way, who might know something about the lay of the land around there."

Stuart Woods was lost in thought for a moment, then said, "I know of a lady in Creal Springs who might know something. She grew up around there, and if anybody knows anything about Creal Springs, it would probably be her. Her name is Olivia Shotwell. Her daddy was Chief of Police in Creal Springs during the "roaring twenties". She might know things we don't. Couldn't hurt to try her. I knew her from church years ago. She used to live around here and she taught grade school. After she retired, she moved back to Creal Springs. Never did get married. She lives in a nursing home in Creal Springs. In fact, I think she owns that nursing home. Not as fancy as this place, I might add." With that, he left the room.

Howard patted Elizabeth's hand and said, "I'm glad you came by. I certainly enjoyed our visit. Sometimes my days go by rather slowly. If I think of anything else that might help you find this lost train, I'll let you know." "Thank you, Mr Bailey." With that, she stood up and left.

That next Saturday, Elizabeth and Dan left the boys with a sitter, and drove to Creal Springs. They found the nursing home easily, as it was on the main route thru town. Olivia Shotwell was a tall, thin woman who carried herself regally, She was a very well mannered lady, in the southern bell fashion. Elizabeth guessed she must have been in her early eighties. She had a private room decorated with things she must have brought with her from her former home. Several rows of old framed photos lined one wall. Olivia Shotwell was reserved at first but quickly warmed up to Elizabeth and Dan. "My father was the police chief here for a number of years. I was a little girl, but I remember lots of goings on in this town back then. My daddy used to tell me stories about the way our little Creal Springs used to be before I came along. Way back then, downtown was a place where people came to do their shopping every Friday night and Saturday. There were more churches than there are now, and lots more people and houses. There were some really beautiful homes. In the summertime, folks would entertain on their front porches in the evenings, and you'd see families strolling down the sidewalks and speaking to each other. It was almost like living in a story book." She sighed. "It's as if I'm talking about two different towns, then and now. Creal Springs has been thru a lot. On Friday nights and all day Saturday, my daddy would say, you couldn't hardly find a place to park your model T. By that time horses and their buggies had to be tied up on the side streets, so as not to spook the horses if one of the cars backfired, and cars seemed to do that a lot back then. And there was more room for the cars to park on the main road thru town."

She gestured with her hands, "All of the area you see around here was taken up by stores of every kind, catering to not only the folks from around here, but the ones who came to get 'the cure' at the Ozark Hotel. Those were heady times, all right." Elizabeth stood near the wall of old framed photos, examining each one, while Dan sat in a recliner facing Olivia Shotwell.

"Miss Shotwell," Dan began but was cut off quickly. "We're all grown ups here, so, please call me Olivia," she insisted. Dan began again, "Olivia, we're interested in some history you might know about. We're looking into a coalmine payroll train that was robbed. You might have heard about it? The train, along with the money was never found."

Olivia said, "That was before my time, but I recall reading something about that train. It happened about the same time the Ozark Hotel burned down for the second time. The train robbery didn't get as much publicity as the hotel burning down did. If I remember right, at the time there were quite a few rich and some famous people staying at the hotel to get the 'cure'. Even the president was here at least once. I remember seeing headlines about those rich and famous people watching their fancy clothes and jewels burn up in the hotel, while they were standing out there on the street in their underwear like everybody else and looking for a bed to sleep in after the hotel burned down, before they all could go back to where ever they came from on the train or by motorcar. I think people forgot about the payroll train pretty quick. Mine owners were all considered to be pretty rich in those days and losing a payroll just didn't impress people too much, although we felt sorry for the miners. Most of them lived from hand to mouth, or you might say paycheck to paycheck. And as you know, they never rebuilt the hotel. It had already burned down once before and had been rebuilt. After that, Creal Springs started to slowly fold in on itself. It wasn't like it used to be. There weren't many jobs to be had, so when kids grew up around here they just left, and didn't come back, and pretty soon, here we are, talking about the way things used to be." She looked at her watch and stood up. "I have some guests coming in a few minutes to see a room I have available, so I really must excuse myself." She showed them to the door. "I wish I could help you more. If you have more questions, please stop by and see me. I don't get too many visitors anymore." They thanked her and left.

As they drove along each street, they gazed upon house after house that was in need of repair. It was as if the people had given up on the community and were letting nature reclaim the land. Sidewalks were cracked, vacant lots were chest high with weeds, and some streets that were paved were slowly becoming gravel roads again. A map they had purchased from the Williamson county Historical Society guided them thru the little city, and detailed where many old buildings had once stood, including the famous Ozark Hotel. According to the map, the grand old hotel had perched upon a rise near the edge of town. Several run down old houses stood there, now.

Dan said, "Close your eyes and let yourself go back almost a hundred years ago, and try to get a feel for the hustle and bustle that must have gone on here." He gestured with his hands. "I can see a model T coming into town along the dirt road that was main street here. I can see it bouncing over ruts and jouncing the people riding in it as they looked for a place to park and do their shopping. They were dressed up in their finery. I can almost smell the stables where the horses were kept just over there," he indicated a street to his left, "and buggies lined up there, too. Kinda stinks ,too" Elizabeth laughed, then poked him in the ribs. "People going everywhere. Towards sunset, a lot of people would be heading home, but then, quite a few were staying at the two hotels in town, and electric lights were coming on everywhere, on street lamps and in stores. It must have been quite a sight." Elizabeth was staring at him.

"What?" Dan looked perplexed. "Did I say something wrong?"

"No, not at all. In fact, you sound like a tour guide. You really were getting into the scene, as it were. I'm impressed."

"Well, that's what I think it must have looked like, anyway." They drove home.

*   *   *   *   *   *   *

The next day was Sunday. After church and lunch, Dan and Elizabeth drove back to the nursing home in Carterville and spoke to Howard Bailey again. Stuart Woods was sitting next to him. They recounted their talk with Olivia Shotwell.

Elizabeth turned to Dan Flatt and said, "Did you look at those photos on the wall In Olivia's room?"

Dan shook his head. "I looked at them, but not closely. Why?"

"One of the photos was of the hotel. Did the railroad run past the hotel? Did the train stop at the hotel? It looks like the hotel was built up on a hill."

Stuart Woods thought for a moment, then said, "Don't go away. I want to talk to somebody for moment." With that, he stood up and left the room. Howard Bailey and Elizabeth made small talk for a few moments, until Stuart Woods returned, pushing a much older black man in a wheelchair. Stuart Woods introduced them all to Benjamin Martin. "Benny has something to tell you folks," said Stuart Woods.

Benny cleared his throat. "When I was growing up in Creal Springs, my daddy worked as a porter at the Ozark. Man, she was a beautiful place to behold!" His eyes glistened as he spoke of the hotel like he would a person. "The folks that would come there to get 'the cure' as they called it, came by the train loads. Yessir. Them trains ran into and out of Creal Springs several times every day, bringing folk from all over the country. Them trains would stop right in front of the hotel. My daddy said that even President Coolidge stayed there for a couple of days."

"Benny," admonished Stuart Woods, "I grew up in Creal and I never heard of no president ever coming to the Ozark. You sure you're not embellishing things just a little bit?"

"No sir, mister Stuart, not one bit. My daddy 'tol me all about it. That train pulled right under the hotel on a special siding and stayed there until the big man was ready to leave."

"Wait a minute," said Howard Bailey. "You said it pulled under the hotel?"

"Yessir, that's what I said," said Benny Martin. "The hotel had a little spur running from just east of the hotel to right underneath of it. That way, rich or famous folks wouldn't need to be seen coming here for the cure. That way they could avoid the gossip. Lots of things white folks don't know about that us people of color know ALL about. Yessir." Benny looked pleased with himself.

They all sat and stared at each other. "But the hotel is long gone now. I never saw any train tracks back there, and I grew up playing all over Creal," said Stuart.

Benny looked at him with his big brown eyes, "You ever see any railroad tracks at all in Creal?"

"Well no. I know there were some, but that was before my time."

Benny went on, "I got a scrapbook in my room, with pictures my daddy took of the hotel way back then. That's around 1915 or so. You want to look at it?"

Stuart Woods wheeled Benny Martin out of the lounge and back to his room.

"The hotel burned down the first time during World War One," said Howard Bailey. "That much I know about the history of Creal Springs. "I learned that when I was a kid in school. Had to do a paper on local history, and I picked out Creal Springs. Did you know there were two hotels and even a college there?"

"Creal Springs was THE place to be for a while," Howard went on. "The coming of paved roads meant people didn't have to travel on trains as much, so many of the local railroads went belly up. Still, there were some railroads running up to Carterville and the mines around there as late as the 1940's."

Presently, Stuart Woods and Benny Martin came back, with a large scrapbook on his lap as Stuart Woods wheeled him into position next to Howard Bailey and Elizabeth. Benny Martin sat up a little straighter, proud that he could show them his prized possession. He gently opened the book as the others gathered around, and turned the pages slowly. Then he pointed a long boney finger at a man standing in front of the hotel in the photo. "That's my daddy." Then he turned more pages and then pointed again.

"That's him on the steps of the hotel. And this picture, "he turned another page, "is the train I was tellin' you all about, UNDERNEATH the hotel. That's the President's train, right there."

They all looked at each other.

Stuart Woods stuttered. "I'll be damned. But Benny, that's all gone now. There's nothing there. It's a city park now. Kids play on swings where that hotel once was. I don't see how this could help find a missing train."

Benny Martin sighed. "I wanted to show this to somebody for a long time. And today's the day. That's all I got to say. Now you folks know what I know." He turned his wheelchair around and headed slowly for the door, the album on his lap. Then he swung around and faced them. "You know that hotel burned down twice. Nobody knows why it burned down the second time, but it did. Makes me wonder if somebody burned it down."

Dan said, "Benny, do you know the date the hotel burned down the second time?"

Benny said, "I wrote it down on the back of the photo I took of the ashes. June 24, 1927."

Dan said, "That's the day after the train was stolen. I wonder if the train itself had anything to do with the fire?"

"You mean the train could be buried under the park in a tunnel?" said Elizabeth.

"Preposterous!" said Stuart Woods. Howard Bailey didn't say anything.

"Wait a minute Benny!" said Howard Bailey. "Wouldn't somebody have seen the train in the tunnel? Even if the hotel burned down?"

"I thought about that, too," said Benny. "But I was told by my daddy that when the fire started it was in the middle of the night, and the hotel she just went WOOSH and the fire went everywhere. Folks was hollerin' and screamin' and runnin' around like they was crazy and you know, one thing the city of Creal Springs never got around to having was a fire department. So nobody knew what to do. My daddy said he just cried as that big beautiful hotel burned down, 'cause his job burned down, too. The hotel just collapsed into a big heap, and that probably filled up the tunnel underneath of it. If there had been a train in the tunnel, why, it would have been buried right along with the hotel. That is, if there really is a train under in there at all. I never heard one way or another if there was one. Yessir, " he smiled a toothless grin at the group gathered in the room, "y'all got yourselves a real mystery." He wheeled himself out of sight down the hall.

That evening, over hot chocolate in the kitchen, Elizabeth related to Dan Flatt what she had learned that day about the tunnel under the hotel. Mason started jumping up and down, "See, I TOLD you it would be there. Let's go dig it up! Can we, Mom?"

Elizabeth laughed and said, "We have to think about this a lot. That land belongs to somebody, if not the city of Creal Springs, and we can't just go digging up the city park without permission." She looked at Dan Flatt, who was deep in thought. "I have an idea," he said, "but I want to do some checking before I say anything more. So, I'll say goodnight and I'll see you all tomorrow," he looked at Elizabeth, then at the boys, "If that's ok with your mom?" The boys looked at Elizabeth.

"What do you think guys, should we invite him back again?" she asked. "Yeah!" said Mason."But only if he doesn't keep kissing you all the time when you think we're not looking," said Mikey. They all got a good laugh out of that.

Chapter Eleven

An old worn out box truck, purchased for next to nothing from U-Haul, cruised the side streets of Marion. Three young men, in their early twenties, one of which was Junior Gulledge, were looking for something they could steal and quickly convert to cash. The driver of the truck, Wayman Smith and Peanut had invited Junior along tonight because they knew he needed cash to repay the bail bond he inherited when he was picked up for burglary in Carterville. Wayman was a little over six feet tall, and skinny as a rail. Peanut was a foot shorter and skinny, too. In high school Peanut had excelled in track. And in his career as a burglar, his exceptional speed had saved his butt more that once. So, tonight the three of them were hoping to score at least once if not two or three times.

They had been cruising the county back roads and small towns for a week now, with pretty good results. Junior was excited about making some extra cash. He was thinking he might have found a new line of work.

Tonight they all wore dark colored t-shirts and jeans, all the easier to blend into the darkness with. Junior rode on the passenger side of the truck; Peanut rode in the middle since he was the smallest of the three. Junior peered at something up ahead then said, "Slow down. I think we got something here." He was looking at a four wheeler Honda sitting off by itself away from the house and garage. They cruised by and turned around at the next intersection. They came back slowly with their lights off. Junior and Peanut slid out of the truck and ran silently towards the four-wheeler. Just before they reached the Honda, a dog started yapping furiously by the garage. They made an immediate about face and jumped into the back of the truck as Wayman picked up speed, running without lights.

"Shit! That would have been a good one, too," said Junior. "Did you get a look at that dog?"

"Naw, I was haulin' my ass back to the truck as fast as I could, so I didn't take time to make friends with no dog," said Peanut. "With my luck he would have been a German Shepard."

"Sounded to me like a Pomeranian," They all got a laugh at that as they drove out of Marion and headed for Johnston City.

There, they cruised the town and found the city cop having coffee at McDonalds with the county police. "Now's the time, boys, since we know where the cops is at," Wayman said. They started on the outskirts of town and hit paydirt on the first street. They loaded up a Honda four-wheeler and a chain saw, then headed out of town on back roads to unload. Their hidey hole was an old farmstead that Wayman had rented for cash a few months back. Not the land, just the house and outbuildings. The grown children of the now deceased couple that had owned the farm lived in town now, and were just glad to get some rent from the buildings they thought would have to be torn down someday.

Wayman drove the truck into the old barn and they unloaded their haul, and put the stolen goods alongside several other interesting items: a jon boat and motor on a trailer, a couple of garden tillers, and another four wheeler similar to the Honda they found tonight. Also, a funny looking john Deere garden tractor with a pink hood instead of a green hood was a part of the haul. It came from a gray house on the edge of Carterville. This was payback from Junior. The tractor came from Elizabeth Jenning's house. She had left it in the yard near the highway where she had stopped mowing the evening before. After they picked up the John Deere, they headed back in the country to Wayman's rental house.

"I figure our take should be around two thousand, give or take a couple hundred," said Wayman. "I think we have enough to call the guys in Missouri and tell 'em to come and get this stuff.

"Hold out for as much as you can," said Junior Gulledge. "I really need that money and I need it soon as I can get it, ya know?"

"OK, man, I'll call them today and have them come over as soon as possible," said Wayman.

Chapter Twelve

The morning sun was climbing steadily into a beautiful blue sky when Elizabeth shooed her boys into the car and drove out of the driveway. Something was nagging at her brain but she couldn't put her finger on it. After dropping the boys off at the sitter, she headed for the hospital. She was examining a patient's chart when it popped into her mind that her garden tractor wasn't out in the yard where she had left it. She made a mental note to check it out when she got home.

That evening, as she pulled into the driveway with her boys, she wandered out into the front yard and looked at the spot where she had left the tractor. That was odd. There were tracks leading to the road. Had somebody taken her funky looking green tractor with the pink hood? She had painted the hood herself. Rust had begun showing up on parts of the hood of the old tractor and rather than repaint it with expensive John Deere paint, she elected to use some spray paint she had found in her garage. Thus, she had a pink hood. She was only teased about it for a little while. Well, a few months. She went into the house and called the police dept.

"I think somebody took my nearly antique John Deere garden tractor," she told the police clerk. "It can't be worth much, but why on earth would anybody steal that thing?" The clerk told her that there had been a rash of thefts in the last two weeks around the county, but so far, there no leads.

The last thing Elizabeth wanted to do was use a push mower on her big yard. She found the weekly Carterville paper and looked up an ad she remembered for lawn services. There was no answer, so she left a message and hung up.

Chapter Thirteen

Early the next morning, an old semi tractor pulling a box trailer pulled into the yard at Wayman's house, and the driver tapped lightly on the air horn. The boys came out of the house and Wayman gave a high-five to the driver, a middle aged guy missing a few teeth from rural Missouri who went by the name of Buddy.

He hooked his hands into his bib overalls as he looked over the loot stashed in the barn and lit a cigarette and was deep in thought for a moment. "Looks pretty good to me. I can move all this stuff. Twenty five hundred for what 'cha got here." He looked at Wayman, then the others.

"That'll do fine by me," said Wayman, nodding his head. Buddy pulled a roll out of his pocket and peeled off enough to cover the purchase. They loaded everything up in the truck and stood around in the yard as Buddy pulled away.

"Well boys," Wayman said, "Time to split things up." He gave each boy his cut and stuffed his back into his pocket.

"Wayman, this was just like Christmas. I never made this much money this quick," Junior said, "But it's not nearly enough to get me out of hock. I need more than this." They decided to go out again that evening and try a different area this time. When the sun started setting, the three boys piled into Wayman's old U-Haul and headed for Harrisburg.

"I got a funny feeling about this town," Junior said. "Folks in Saline county are known to shoot first and call the cops last. I don't want nothing to do with guns."

"Well," said Peanut, "We'll just have to be quicker. I saw you run away from that German Shepard. You could have won a medal on that one." Junior wasn't convinced.

Harrisburg residents seemed to know something was afoot, and they found little to choose from around there. They cruised on to Eldorado and had better luck. A four wheeler found its way into their truck, as did a small dirt bike motorcycle. Another attempt wasn't so fruitful. As they tried to unlock a shed door, a porchlight came on and a man, wearing only boxer shorts, ran out of the house yelling, pointing with a shotgun. He fired twice and they fled, but not before Junior and Wayman each got hit with buckshot pellets in the back and rear end. They raced back to Wayman's house, with Peanut driving. Junior and Wayman weren't hurt badly, but they were bleeding and every bump caused them to cuss at Peanut and tell him to avoid the potholes in the road. As if Peanut could see them in time at night on a county road that was mostly bumps anyway.

They unloaded their meager haul into the barn and limped back into the house. Junior tried to sit but found he did much better if he lay on his side on the sofa. Wayman moaned a lot as he lay on his bed. Junior asked Peanut to look at his butt and Peanut said no way was he gonna look at Juniors ass, but after a few threats, Peanut finally agreed reluctantly, to take a peek.

Junior slid his jeans down carefully and Peanut said "Aw man, it's just a couple of little bitty holes. You want me to dig them pellets out?' Junior said yes.

Peanut, while not exactly an EMT, used a small pair of needle nosed pliers from Wayman's toolbox, after he'd ran them under hot water for a couple of minutes.

When it was Junior's turn, he tensed up and yelled thru gritted teeth as Peanut dug around for the little pieces of buckshot, and proudly held one up for Junior to see. Junior wasn't impressed. "Are you done?" he said.

"Naw, got one more is all I can see. Hang on, here we go."

Once more Junior let out a long muffled groan. Peanut held up another pellet. "I better put a bandaid on those holes". As he dropped each pellet on a plate, he felt like a doctor he'd seen on TV. Peanut went to check on Wayman. He was asleep.

That night they brought home a four wheeler, a garden tiller and two bicycles. Even in their wounded condition, they were back in business.

Chapter Fourteen

When they were in high school and going steady, during the summer, Dan would pick up Elizabeth at her grandmother's house, then once at his little country airstrip, they would strap themselves into his little ultralight and go flying. They would fly until they needed gas, then land on a highway and coast into the nearest gas station to get a fill up, much to the shock and total surprise of the gas station owner and their patrons. So when Dan asked her if she'd like to go for a flight, she jumped at the chance. She dropped the boys off at the sitter and they were on their way. She told Dan that one of these days, he would need to take each boy flying or the boys would set up a howl. Dan just smiled. He'd been planning to ask her if he could take the boys flying, and now she'd just given him a green light. The little plane taxied to the edge of Dan's pasture, and he pointed it down the mowed strip of the pasture. He stood on the brakes, as the motor wound up to a scream, then let go of the brakes and steered the plane until the rudder took effect. A few seconds after that, he pulled back on the stick and they leaped into the air. They were off! The Quicksilver ultralight carried Dan and Elizabeth serenely over the treetops. They flew south and east, towards the more hilly part of Southern Illinois, Dan's favorite area to fly over, and as they flew on they swooped down to skim cornfields, then to the edges of pastures, then up and over the trees again. Elizabeth loved this. As long as the engine didn't quit, which it never had, thank goodness.

They flew in a lazy arc around Southern Illinois, checking out little towns and hamlets as they flew on and on. Their flight was into the second hour when Dan pointed to a little combination gas station and grocery store. At first, Elizabeth didn't understand what Dan was doing with his hands until he smacked the gas tank above their head. "We need gas!" He mouthed and grinned. Then suddenly Elizabeth understood. They were going to land on the highway just down from a country gas station that was set back into the trees alongside the highway by itself. Her eyes grew wide as they made a wide circle around the store a couple of times, until a pick up truck pulled away from the only gas pump.

Dan pointed the nose down and they dropped below the treetops and touched the asphalt roadway, with the centerline passing under the nosewheel. They touched down lightly.

Dan shut off the engine as they left the highway and coasted to a stop across the dusty gravel parking lot next to the gas pump. Dan unbuckled his seatbelt and left Elizabeth sitting in the plane as he swiped his credit card and started filling the gas tank. The owner came around the building, wiping his hands on an oily rag as he took in the strange sight of a brightly colored airplane parked at his gas pump.

Presently a couple of cars pulled into the drive and two older couples piled out to gaze at the airplane. Just then Elizabeth unbuckled her seatbelt and asked where the ladies room was. The owner pointed inside "All the way back to the pizza counter, then left. You'll see it. Says Ladies on it." As Elizabeth walked out of the store, Dan said, "Hey, I'm hungry, and they sell pizza here. Why don't we have lunch?

He finished filling the plane. They pushed the plane away from the pumps, and parked it next to the store. Half an hour later, they wiped their hands on napkins, finished their sodas and pulled the ultralight from its parking spot. A touch of the starter and the little plane shook itself as the motor revved up. They strapped themselves in and waved at the small crowd that had assembled. Dan steered the plane to the edge of the highway, looked both ways then pulled out to the centerline and pointed the plane down the highway. He pushed the throttle all the way forward and the plane practically leaped off the ground. Just in time, too, because a gravel truck came up over a hill as they gained altitude. The driver of the truck stared openmouthed as they passed over him with only a few feet to spare. They were flying again!

The Ohio river sparkled like a glittering ribbon in the distance, so they aimed for the river. They followed the shoreline for a while, waving at people fishing on the banks. Dan headed out over the river towards a small island. He dropped lower and lower until they were just a few feet above the sandbar that surrounded the island. Something ahead caught his attention and he moved out over the water about ten feet from shore, as they flew by a young couple frantically trying to get their bathing suits back on. Dan climbed a little and waggled his wings, laughing. Elizabeth punched him on the arm, giving him a stern look that dissolved into a big grin. She then shook her head as they flew on.

Soon they turned back north towards home. The sun was still high enough to guide them but the day had lost some of its warmth and soon it would become chilly. As they flew over Creal Springs, Dan picked out an old railroad bed to follow back towards home. Farm after farm disappeared behind them. Another farm appeared ahead, but this one looked rundown, and uncared for. As they passed overhead, Elizabeth grabbed Dan's arm and mouthed "turn around". She made a circling motion with her hand, so Dan put the plane into a left turn to bring them back around over the farm. Elizabeth peered intently at something as they flew over the farm again, then she sat back and said nothing as they flew on towards home.

The trip from the farm to the landing strip had taken only a few minutes. When they landed, and the engine had shut off, he said, "What was all that circling around that farmhouse for back there?"

"That was my garden tractor back there."

"Are you sure?"

She nodded her head

"Absolutely positive that was yours?"

"One hundred and ten percent."

"Well, how many garden tractors have a pink hood painted where it should have been green? Now, are we going to go get my tractor back?"

"Yep, just as soon as I call the sheriff." Dan replied, digging out his cell phone. He made the call and told the sheriff 's deputy who answered about finding the garden tractor from the air. The deputy seemed skeptical.

Dan hung up, a frown on his face. "What's the matter" asked Elizabeth. "Well, it's not exactly a murder or missing persons case, so they'll have somebody swing by the farm eventually." Elizabeth planted her hands on her hips. "I think we should maybe cruise by that farm ourselves. Can we?" she looked up at Dan. They hopped into his jeep and headed for Carterville.

* * * * *

When the little ultralight suddenly began to turn around and come back, Junior yelled, "Everybody hide!"

In a few seconds the plane had swooped overhead again and headed north along the old railroad trackbed.

"I wonder what in hell they were looking for?" said Peanut. Junior looked around and saw the garden tractor with the funny pink hood sitting out in the middle of the yard, along with several other tractors and 4-wheelers.

"Oh, shit. Oh, shit, oh shit. Damn!" Junior was thinking furiously, holding his head with both hands, walking in circles. "I think they was looking for that pink tractor. I just bet they were. Damn, boys, we gotta move this stuff out of here now!" Junior was so agitated he was hopping around like he was high on something.

Peanut backed his truck up to the nearest garden tractor and they began loading everything they could onto the back of the truck. The yard was empty, but the truck was overloaded and the front wheels of the truck barely touched the dirt. Peanut didn't like the looks of that. He cocked his head a little, while looking at the overloaded back. He jumped onto the pile of stolen equipment and moved a 4-wheeler towards the front. Then he jumped off the truck and cocked his head again. There! Now the truck would ride ok. The front of the truck sat more squarely on the ground. Otherwise, when he turned the front wheels, nothing would have happened; the truck would have continued on down the road. Everything looked better now. They pulled a tarp over the load and lashed it down with baling wire and drove out of the driveway towards Missouri.

* * * * *

Dan pulled his Jeep into his mother's driveway and jumped out. "I'll only be a minute," he said, as he ran up the steps onto the porch and thru the front door.

"Hi mom," he yelled as he bounded up the inside staircase to his room. He came back out a moment later with his 12gauge shotgun, a Christmas gift from his dad upon turning fifteen years old.

"Want some cookies?" his mom asked, standing in the hallway to the kitchen. "They've only been out of the oven about half an hour."

"Well," Dan said, hesitating, "Maybe only a half dozen or so. Elizabeth is with me and we need to get going."

"Will you be back for supper?" she said, as she filled a paper sack with fresh baked chocolate chip cookies.

"I don't know, you probably shouldn't wait on me," he said over his shoulder as he hurried out the door and back to the idling Jeep. His mom followed him out on the porch and waved at Elizabeth. "You two have fun, but be careful with that gun!" she yelled as they drove off. She wiped her hands on her apron and went back inside, happy to see the two of them together again after all these years. She smiled and went back to her kitchen.

The trip to Creal Springs seemed to take forever to Elizabeth. She glanced over at Dan Flatt who, despite a menacing set to his face, otherwise managed to give her hand a quick squeeze.

"Scared?" he asked over the rush of air around the Jeep. "Maybe. What if they have guns, too?" Dan turned and stared at her for a long second then turned his attention back to the road. "I'm not looking to get into a gunfight with those guys. We don't even know how many there are. If they start shooting at us, we'll get out of there and call the police again. " 'Shots fired' ought to bring every cop for miles around."

Dan checked out the road to the farm on Google Earth before they left, and he found the road easily. Over the railroad tracks and then about a mile or so brought them to the farm. With the dense treeline and overhanging foliage, they were able to drive up to the entrance to the farm without being noticed. However, the farm was deserted. No vehicles were in sight. They slowly drove up the driveway to the house. Nothing stirred. Dan eased out of the Jeep, then reached behind the front seat and pulled out the shotgun, keeping it pointed down towards the ground. He motioned to Elizabeth to stay in the Jeep as he first checked out the barn, then circled around the house.

"Nobody's here," he yelled at her from back of the house.

She swung her legs out of the Jeep and joined him at the sidewalk in front of the house. The screen door was standing open and the front door had not been pulled shut. Dan pushed the door open with his foot and called out "Anybody here? Hello? I've got your mail!" Nothing moved. They slowly entered what was the living room. The place was a mess. Fast food wrappers littered the floors and tables. Empty beer cans stood on the dining room table, along with empty pizza boxes.

They checked out the rest of the house downstairs, including a kitchen that reeked of stale food. "I wonder how they could live like this?" said Elizabeth.

As they prepared to check out the upstairs, a voice behind them said "Guess my renters are gone." Dan whirled around, bringing the shotgun up as he spun, only to find a grizzled old man in bib overalls standing in the doorway, his long skinny arms hanging down at his sides. Dan quickly lowered the gun.

"You folks don't look like you belong to them boys," said the old man.

"No" Dan said," We're trying to find a garden tractor we think they stole from Elizabeth here."

The old man scratched his head. "I checked up on these boys once in a while. Don't believe they ever knew I was around. I can be pretty quiet when I want to be," he grinned, showing a few missing teeth. He held out his hand, "Name's Everett Morgan."

Dan shook his hand and introduced Elizabeth. After a quick hand-shake, she said "My garden tractor had a pink spot on the hood. Have you seen it here?"

"I believe I did see one like that. There was a whole bunch of stuff out in the yard by the barn a couple of days ago. You say it belongs to you?"

She nodded. "It was stolen from my backyard several days ago."

The old man stared at the ground for a moment, then looked at them. "I saw a truck here once, a few days ago. It was a big truck, you know a tractor and trailer rig. It pulled into the driveway and right away, they began loading everything they had into the trailer. It had a ramp they could roll stuff right up into the truck. Didn't take them no time at all to load that stuff up."

"Do you remember who owned the truck? Was there a name on the door?" asked Dan.

"I supposed there was, but I wasn't close enough to be able to read it. I do remember something, though."

"What was that?" asked Elizabeth.

"It had a Missouri license plate on the front of the truck," said the old man. They thanked him and as they were about to leave, a sheriff's car pulled into the drive. They explained to the short round deputy who they were and why they had called. The deputy hitched up his gunbelt a couple of times, took some notes and wandered around the barn, then looked inside the house.

"Who ever was here, didn't leave much behind," said the deputy. "They must have been planning to make a fast getaway, I think."

"How long did they live here?" asked Elizabeth. The old man said he thought they were here going on four months. "They never made much fuss over anything. They paid the rent in advance on the first of every month, in cash, the way I like it. No need to mess with cashing no checks, which could bounce. Know what I mean?" They all nodded.

"I wonder if they ever got any mail," said Dan. I think I'll look in the mailbox. "Here, let me," said the Deputy. They watched as he walked across the road to a lone mailbox mounted on a low fencepost. He stood to one side as he opened the door. "Had a case one time," said the deputy, "guy wanted to get back at his ex wife for divorcing him, so he planted a couple of M80 firecrackers in the mailbox. If she hadn't done the same thing I just did, we would have been after him for murder. Instead, he just got ten years in prison for attempted murder."

He pulled out a handful of mail and sorted thru it. "Junk mail, addressed to box holder. Nothing with a name on it. He stuffed it back into the mailbox and crossed over the road to them again, standing in the hot sun. "Guess I'll go file my report." To Dan he said "Careful where you point that shotgun." Dan nodded. It was pointed at the ground. The deputy got back in his car and left.

The old man said, "Them boys are paid up until the end of the month. You never know, they might be back."

Chapter Fifteen

That evening, Dan Flatt had supper with Elizabeth and the boys. Times like this made him think hard about a life with the four of them together.

"Supper was just about perfect," said Dan as Elizabeth sat down next to him on the porch swing.

"What do you mean, 'just about' mister?" she said, playfully poking him in the ribs.

"Well you always have to leave a little room for improvement." "Hmmm. Next time, you can cook for the four of us. "Not a problem," said Dan. "I happen to know where there is a perfectly good deli." That got him another poke. "Hey, cut it out!" She dug at his ribs again. They were laughing and poking at each other, when the front door flew open and the two boys jumped onto the swing and began tickling both of them. Elizabeth screamed and laughed at the same time. Finally they all settled down after Dan promised to take them all to the Dairy Queen for ice cream cones.

Later, as they sat around a table outside in the summer night at the DQ, licking their cones. Dan said, "Isn't there such a thing as ground radar? Seems like I've heard of it before."

"I wonder if coal mines use something like that," said Elizabeth. "If so, you could ask Bruce Talley. I'll be he would know. Or else he'd know someone who would know."

"Bruce Talley. Who is he?"

"He's an old guy who lives out near the park. He used to be a coal mine inspector before he retired. He's pretty smart. At least he wants people to think he's pretty smart."

The next morning, Dan looked up Bruce Talley's phone number in the phone book at his mom's house. It rang several times, but no one answered. He asked his mom about Bruce Talley and she knew him. She gave him directions to his place with a warning to make lots of noise, lest he get a load of buckshot for a greeting.

Bruce Talley lived just north of the city park, in a patch of forest thick with undergrowth. A narrow path led up a hill from a weather beaten mailbox. Dan Flatt, shuffled his feet in the gravel, and made as much noise as he could without singing as he walked up the path. About a hundred feet in from the mailbox, the path made a turn and around the turn he pulled up short to find a wizened old man with spikey white hair holding a shotgun. "That's far enough," said the old man.

"I hope you're Bruce Talley, or else I'm in big trouble, said Dan. The old man stared at Dan for a moment, then pointed the shotgun at the ground, and eased off the hammer. "You remind me of a kid that I used to see around here years ago."

"My name is Dan Flatt. My dad was Herman Flatt, the postmaster, and my mom is Vera Flatt. We lived over by the Methodist church. My mom still lives there.

"I know her, but I don't know you." He sat the stock of the gun on the ground and relaxed a little. "Why are you looking for me?"

"I understand you were a coal mine inspector once upon a time. I came to ask you about ground radar."

"What about it?

"Well, can you find something buried underground? Maybe fifty feet down?"

Bruce tally pursed his lips. "Yeah, you probably could. What are you looking for?"

"A train."

That brought a huge laugh from the old man. "You lose a train? Around here?"

"If you'll put that shotgun away, I'll tell you about my thoughts concerning a train."

He looked at Dan for a long moment then said, "I need a drink. Follow me." He led the way along the path to a ramshackle house. It was little more than a cabin, consisting of two bedrooms, a sitting room, a kitchen and a tiny bath. Cozy but small. A compact wood stove in the middle of the cabin looked like it was big enough to heat the whole place in the winter time.

They sat at a table for two and Bruce Talley offered Dan iced tea. The two men sipped their drinks and eyed each other. Presently, Bruce Talley said, "OK, tell me about your train." He chuckled. "You really lost a train? A real train?"

Dan told him about the missing coal mine payroll train from the 1920's. Bruce got up from the table and returned with a handsome photo book on the history of Carterville. He thumbed thru page after page, then turned the book around and showed the photo to Dan.

"This the train you're looking for?" The photo showed a gleaming coal fired locomotive, A Baldwin 2-4-2, numbered that way because of two small wheels under the front of the locomotive, then four big drive wheels, then two smaller wheels under the cab of the locomotive, pulling a coal tender, and a long ornate well shielded car, with the words Wells Fargo & Company in gold leaf running the length of the car above the windows and door. Five men stood next to the train. One man was obviously the engineer, and next to him was the fireman. The other three wore badges displayed on the outside of their suit coats.

Security guards. Each carried a shotgun crooked in their arm. Dan wondered which one was Elizabeth's Great Grandfather. From the looks of the men in the photo, none of them had the slightest idea that they would disappear into history without a trace. He placed his finger on the photo on the page.

"That's the one. It just disappeared into thin air. I have an idea I want to check out but I need a radar unit, if it will do what I've heard they will do." "So I'm guessing you think its buried somewhere around here. Well, it would take a hell of a big hole to bury a train like that. But the ground penetrating radar? I know where one is. It doesn't get used much. You would probably have to make a donation to the group that owns it, in order to use it."

"I don't know anything about how it operates. I'm in the dark about that. Do you know of someone who could run the thing?"

"Yeah," said Bruce Talley. "Me."

"You?" Dan looked at the old man. "You would do this for me? I don't have any money to speak of. I can't hire you, or anything like that."

"Well, I suppose I could go along with you as a consultant on this project."

He sat back in his chair. "Well, this would be the most fun I've had in a few years. So, where are you going to look for this train at?"

Dan said, "You get the machine and I'll tell you more when we're on the way to the site. I don't want any nosy media following us around. Or any treasure hunters. This is probably a wild goose chase. I'm doing this for my girlfriend, so she can clear her great grandfathers name. That's all."

"OK." The old man drained his tea, then picked up their glasses and laid them in the sink. "Give me your number and I'll call you when I get the unit. If I get the unit."

Chapter Sixteen

A couple of days later, Dan received a call from Bruce Talley. "I have the unit and we can look for your train whenever you want." Dan and Bruce met for coffee the next morning at a McDonalds. Bruce blew across the top of his coffee cup to cool it down. "Tell me what you know about this train. You got any real facts, not just rumors?"

Bruce said, "I grew up here in Carterville, and so did you. And I have never heard of a train getting hijacked and then having it vanish into thin air. Have you?"

Dan said, "Well, things happen. Then over the years, people either forget about them or the story changes. Do you remember when Lindbergh landed here in Carterville and gave rides before he flew across the Atlantic?"

Bruce cocked his head and looked at him funny. "No way. Where? Here in Carterville?"

"Yep. You know where that old red barn is on South Division Street?

"Yes," said Bruce, slowly. Then a light went on behind his eyes. "That's why there's a 'Lindbergh Lane' there, huh?"

Dan said, "That used to be a big meadow. Hard to picture it now, since it's a big subdivision with houses all over the place out there. See? Things can happen right under your nose and be forgotten in history. So, we have records of the train getting hijacked and people getting shot up. That tells me the story is real enough. Now, all we have to do is continue on and try to figure out where the train is after all these years." He almost said something to Bruce about the money Elizabeth found in her basement, but decided not to.

Dan said, "After doing some research at the Williamson County Historical Society, we've read that on the night it was hijacked, the train was spotted slowly going thru Marion after midnight, with no lights on and it didn't blow its whistle any time. That tells me they were sneaking thru town. Somebody saw it and notified the police, because they thought it was very unusual for a train not to be lit up and making lots of noise with its steam whistle. The cops evidently came up with nothing, according to their police report. Except, the next day, the train robbery was reported in the newspaper. It never got very much attention, because that same day Lindbergh made it across the Atlantic to Paris, and that got the world's attention for a week. And, that same day, the Ozark Hotel in Creal Springs burned down for the second time. So there was a lot going on all at the same time." Dan continued, "So, I have been studying the rail lines that were present at the time from Marion going east and south and I have decided that that train has to be somewhere here in Southern Illinois. It was never reported crossing the Ohio River or the Mississippi, either. And the states keep pretty good track of trains, because the railroads have to pay taxes on their freight every time they cross state lines. And, naturally, the states don't want to lose any money." Bruce said, "Any idea where in Southern Illinois you want to look? I probably won't live long enough for you and me to penetrate every hill south of here with this radar."

"I've flown over every old railroad bed I could find and I came up with nothing. Nothing even remotely resembled a place where you could hide an entire train. So," he paused for a moment, "I think we should look where nobody ever thought of looking." Bruce waited patiently for Dan to finish, but finally he said, "Well?" Dan said, "I think we should start with the Ozark Hotel."

Bruce Talley said, "You know, I never heard about Lindbergh landing here in Carterville, until you told me. And now, you're telling me about this hotel in Creal Springs that burned down. I never heard of it, either. Where have I been when all this stuff was happening?"

Dan opened up his ipad and brought up the internet. Then he called up photos of the Ozark Hotel, and turned the ipad around so Bruce could see the photos.

"That's quite a hotel!" Bruce said.

Dan said, "Yes, and to think it was built twice, and not only that, there, was another hotel in Creal Springs besides the Ozark. And, besides that, there was a hospital and a small college. And, none of those are there now. Amazing. Just amazing."

They decided to start looking in a day or two.

Dan headed home to work on his mother's house a little more.   Shortly after five pm, Dan was still up on a ladder scraping loose paint when a car horn tooted behind him. Scraper in hand, he carefully turned around on the ladder to find Elizabeth and her boys in the car at the curb. "You want something lady?" he yelled at her, grinning from the top of the ladder.

She hollered back, "Why don't you and your mom come over for supper after you get cleaned up? And that includes a shower."

"This is Mom's bridge club night. I was going to have leftovers, so I guess I'll have to come by myself and eat her share. Hey, why can't I just come like this?" She hollered back, "Because I know what you smell like when you've been working hard, which is rare, I'll admit, but I don't want to smell you and not the fried chicken." He waved the scraper at her as they drove off.

Chapter Seventeen

Dan had pictured a ground penetrating radar in his mind as big, bulky and very heavy. He was wrong on all counts. It was more like two laptop computers mounted on a four wheeled contraption that looked sort of like a walker for old folks. They folded it up, then loaded it into the back of Dan's Jeep and headed east on Route 13, then turned south on Route 166 towards Creal Springs. On the way there, Dan explained to Bruce what he wanted to do with the machine. Bruce wasn't impressed.

"You really want to find a whole train?" He asked, incredulous.

"Well, yeah, now that you mention it," said Dan. "What better way to find something big underground that's made mostly of steel than with something that can detect big areas other that rock."

"How far underground?"

"Well, I don't know exactly."   "Well, what *do* you know about this train? Exactly?"

The drive to Creal Springs was not long, about thirty minutes. During that time, Dan and Bruce traded questions about each other. Bruce was intrigued that Dan was a "repo man" but only going after airplanes. He thought that was fascinating, if not dangerous work. "Have you ever been shot at?" Asked Bruce. "Only a couple of times," replied Dan.

"I would be absolutely terrified."

"Well, the thought of being down in a hole in the ground you call a mine and having the earth give off a little tremor, scares the crap out of me!" said Dan.

"Aw, it's nothing really. You get used to the ground moving", said Bruce. "And, of course, there's the lights going out all the time. You always need to have a good battery in your pack. You know, just in case of a cave in and you're down there for a day or two until they dig you out." Bruce grinned slyly at Dan.

Dan gave an involuntary shiver. He decided to change the subject. "How many times have you used this radar thing?"

"Never."

"What? But I thought...You said..."

"No, I said I knew where there was one. I didn't say I knew how to use one. A friend of mine works for Southern Illinois University and they have one that was donated to them in their anthropology department. He signed it out to us for a few days. And he showed me how to use this one yesterday. I've seen them used, so I know which buttons to push and how to read the screen.

Also, there are different antennas used for locating different objects. I brought what I think is the right antenna for our search. As we drive the unit over the ground, if there is a large object buried down there, it will show the outline of the object if we go over the ground enough times, back and forth."

Dan asked, "Will it show anything thru concrete?"

"Yep. This antenna will show concrete as a solid object and the metal from a railroad car as a solid object. If there is only railroad tracks down there, it will find us the tracks and nothing else. Tracks should show up as two straight lines."

"Pretty slick," said Dan. "How do you know all this stuff?" "Well, I stayed at a Holiday Inn Express once." Bruce laughed and Dan just rolled his eyes.

Creal Springs came into view around a bend in the road and they slowed down as they cruised thru town. Bruce consulted a map spread out on his lap as Dan drove slowly along what used to be a busy, but now nearly deserted, main street. A row of brick buildings gave way to a city park built on a hill. The park was also deserted. They pulled into the parking lot and unloaded the radar unit. It resembled a three wheel baby stroller with a laptop mounted near the top of the handles and a metal box about two feet square resting in the "carriage". Bruce fiddled with the handlebar mounted controls a bit then straightened up and announced that he was ready to start scanning. He said OK, Dan, where do we start?"

Dan said "Beats me." He pointed to the hill. Why don't we start at the top and work our way down." He helped Bruce push the radar unit up the hill, then stood back as Bruce powered it up. Bruce looked at Dan and laughed, "It won't hurt you."

Dan nodded his head. "You're the one who has never used it before and you know this how?" The unit gave off a sudden beep and they both jumped. Bruce twisted a knob and said, "Well, now we know it works. It's already found something. Have a look."

The screen was filled with row after row of lines similar to the lines on a heart monitor, only grey instead of green. A solid line running top to bottom moved off the screen as they pushed the buggy forward. They stopped. Dan said, "Did we just roll over a wall or something?" Bruce was studying the screen carefully. "I think so. Let's move on forward and see what we find."

An hour later, they had mapped out what appeared to be part of a foundation, and judging from the size of the foundation, it was the hotel. Bruce reset the penetrating signal several times to several different depths, but nothing else showed up besides the foundation. They were, however, able to map out rooms on the foundation. Nothing of any substance showed up on the screen. There was nothing resembling a train buried under the city park. Frustrated, they called it quits and loaded the radar unit into the Jeep and headed for home.

As early morning daylight took over the darkness, Dan lay in bed and thought about the radar and finding nothing of interest down in Creal

Springs. He had the feeling that they'd missed something, but what? He had an idea.

He pulled into the parking lot of the nursing home and headed inside. The receptionist said the residents were having breakfast and he could go on back to the dining hall. He raised his eyebrows a little and she pointed down the hall and to the right. "Just keep going," she said, "It's a big room." He found the men eating together. Howard Bailey spotted him and waved him over. "Grab that chair from that table over there, drag it over here and join us," he said between forkfuls of scrambled eggs. "Tell us what you've been doing." He waved his fork at Dan. "Find anything yet?"

"In a word, no." Dan said. "But, I'm not done. I just need more ideas." He looked around the table at the old guys staring at him. He outlined what he and Bruce Talley did with the radar. No one commented.

Bennie, the old black man, finally said, "Mr. Dan, where on that hillside did you look?" Dan told him where he and Bruce had started and how they had worked a grid pattern so they wouldn't miss anything.

"Been a long time since I was down to Creal," said Bennie. "My memory ain't always right about things anymore." That started everybody laughing, cackling and razzing each other about their ability to remember things. Dan had an idea. He excused himself and brought his ipad from the Jeep. He turned it on and quickly brought up Google earth, then zoomed in on Creal Springs. He passed the ipad around the table. They took turns examining the image of Creal Springs from the air. He showed them how they could zoom in and out, in order to bring up more detail. When the ipad got to Bennie, he said, "where on this patch of ground did you look?" Dan zoomed the image in. "Right here."

Bennie looked at the ceiling for a moment, then at the faces of each of the circle of old men staring at him, then he looked back at Dan and said, "You know there used to be two big hotels side by side back then, on the east side of Creal Springs?

Dan said, "Two? Side by side?"

"Yep," said Benny, "The Ozark, and the Taylor House Hotel." He handed the ipad back to Dan. "Show me again where on this thing you say you looked." Dan zoomed in more on the patch of land. I thought we'd be better off looking over here by the road."

Bennie replied, "Wern't no road there back then, Mr. Dan. The road was over here. See them buildings in the picture? Draw a line out a ways then start a long slow curve to the south. All that ground past these here buildings was where the hotels were. You need to look over here." He pointed a long bony finger at the side of the screen. " See this here house? That house was built where the other hotel used to be. It was built after the Ozark caught fire. I don't think the tracks ran under all of the hotels. Just the Ozark." Dan held up his hand, and said just a minute, then brought up Google street view. It was as if he had performed a magic trick. All the old guys were stunned. "How 'd you do that?" asked Howard Bailey. "I need to get one of them things!" Dan passed the ipad around the table again. There was the buildings, the empty hillside and the old house. He zoomed in on the house and it showed an empty derelict house slowly falling in on itself. "So this house is where one of the hotels used to be, Bennie?" The old man just nodded. He said "I think you was looking up on the hillside where the Taylor House Hotel used to be."

"Bennie, you want to take a ride down to Creal Springs and guide us around?" Bennie agreed, and Dan said he would pick him up the next morning. Dan called Bruce Talley and told him Bennie would be coming with them the next day. When Dan and Bennie met Bruce at McDonalds, Bruce said "Where's Elizabeth?"

"Poor thing. She has to work."

  "She know what you do for a living?"

He stuffed another bite of eggs into his mouth. "I don't think she has a real good handle on my occupation. I told her I'm an 'aviation relocation specialist'. She just stared at me. I don't think she got the connection."

Bennie paid no attention to them. He was focused on his sausage and egg biscuit.

Chapter Eighteen

The drive to Creal Springs was a short one. Bennie sat in the passenger seat and pointed out changes in the countryside that had happened over the years. Bruce peered out from the back seat. When they drove into Creal Springs, Bennie said "Slow down a little." He seemed confused.

Dan said, "Bennie, when was the last time you were in Creal Springs?" "Nineteen fifty one. Or maybe fifty-two. I left town on a train headed for Detroit, Michigan. I was gonna make me some big money in one of them car factories. That train I got on came right thru there." He pointed at a shallow ravine. He looked around again, then pointed behind the old bank. "The train depot was back there on a side street." He looked around in wonderment. Finally, he pointed at an old building." That was the bank. Everybody banked there. Yessir, that was the bank. That was my bank! I had me a safe deposit box there. All my valuable stuff was in that box. That was a long time ago." He looked around at the vacant lots between what few buildings were still standing. A part of him seemed to shrink even further than his already slight stature. "My god. Everything's gone. All them buildings is just...*gone*." He looked like he'd stepped back in time. "This whole part of town was filled with all kinds of stores. Why, you could buy just about anything your heart desired. Even when I left to go work in Chicago, there was a whole lot more to Creal Springs than just this." His eyes teared up a little. "I grew up here. I never thought Creal would ever look like...this." Look at them houses, why, they're just falling down. They were pretty nice houses when I lived here. And, now...don't nobody care anymore?"

The first thing they did after entering town was to make a stop at the police station. The police station was housed in what used to be a shell gas station. The whole place had been remodeled, the pumps long gone, and the canopy removed. The police chief was a slender young man with a blond haircut sliced off in the style of marines. He was about six feet tall and carried himself in the manner of a recently re-leased soldier. He wore a bored look on his face as they entered the small police station, but perked up when they told him what they wanted to do. They invited him to keep watch as they prowled around the area where the hotels had been.

The young police chief, whose name tag said WILLIS, said "I read up on the history of this town when I was hired, since I didn't grow up here, but this is the first time anybody has ever come around wanting to look for anything. Judging from all the photos I've seen in history books, I would love to have seen this place a hundred years ago! I'll bet the police department was busy back then." Bennie cackled and pointed a boney finger at the young man. "Sonny, a hundred years ago, it would have taken a whole bunch of you guys to keep the peace, es-pecially on Saturday nights!" They all laughed. The police chief said "I don't think anybody will mind you guys tramping around on the hill over there, since most of it is city property, but if I'm with you, it'll look more official." He hitched up his gunbelt. "Give the residents something to talk about, and you know they'll be all over the phone lines just as soon as you guys start looking."

The chief followed them in his squad car to the hillside. No sooner had they all gotten out of their cars than a couple of ladies appeared on their porches, arms crossed, to watch whatever was going on. Their houses were on top of the hillside, and next to their houses was a ramshackle derelict house that was slowly giving way to nature. From all appearances, their houses weren't far behind.

Dan and Bruce explained to the chief about the ground penetrating radar, and how it was supposed to work. Bennie seemed lost in his own thoughts. He ambled about over the hillside as Dan and Bruce systematically covered the area, back and forth in a grid pattern. They worked from the top of the hill to the bottom. After three hours of slow, plodding effort, they were done.

Dan steered the buggy under the shade of a tree. Bruce brought up the computer screen and they watched as he scrolled right to left, back and forth down the hillside. At the bottom of the hill, two lines appeared. "Here's the railroad tracks we found yesterday."

Nothing else of interest showed up underground. They decided to break for lunch. The cop left to make his rounds in the squad car. The three men found a little convenience store with a snack bar across the street from the hillside, and ordered sandwiches and cokes. They were tired. Bennie, however, was full of vigor.

"Bennie, this afternoon, how about YOU push that buggy awhile," said Bruce. Bennie said, "Hey, I'm just a helpless old man. You both are a lot younger that I am. Besides, I think you're looking in the wrong place." He grinned.

Bruce and Dan looked at each other. "What?"

"If we were looking in the wrong place, why didn't you stop us? Said Bruce. Bennie replied: "First of all, you didn't ask. Then again, if you DID ask, well, I could always be wrong," said Bennie. "That old falling down house on the other side of the hill over there, the one next to them old ladies' houses?" They turned around in the booth to stare at the houses on the hillside across the street from the convenience store. They nodded.

"I think that's where the back end of the Ozark Hotel was. The hill is different now, but I think that's where it was. You guys ought to look around that house and see if you can find anything buried around there, like a wall or something."

They finished their lunch. Bennie decided to sit in Dan's Jeep, while they pushed the GPR buggy up the hill towards the old house. One of the ladies who was watching them earlier came out to talk with them.

Up close, she appeared to be in her eighties. She was wearing a threadbare housedress and had curlers in her hair.

"Whatcha all doing there?" she asked.

"Well," said Dan. "We're looking for where the Ozark Hotel used to be. This contraption is like radar that we can see under ground a little ways. We run it back and forth over the ground, and if there is something like a wall or railroad track that's buried under there, we'll see an outline. We're trying to locate some railroad tracks that're buried around here. Possibly a tunnel."

"A tunnel, huh? I don't know about any tunnel, but then, maybe I do. Well, maybe I can help you some," she said. "I've lived in this house for a long time. It was built in the fifties sometime, I think. One day, my late husband was down in the basement and felt some cold air coming around the concrete blocks on the wall of the basement. He removed a couple of blocks and found a hole that the air was coming from. He wasn't interested in the hole, he just wanted to keep the cold air out. He said it might have been from some coal mine that was closed up. You know there were old coal mine shafts underneath the ground all over around here. In fact, once in a while a shaft will just give way. I remember years ago a house just fell in on itself because it was sitting right on top of a mine shaft nobody knew about. They had to tear the house down. Them people that owned the house was mighty mad, too. My husband told me about it and then I forgot all about it until it came back to me just now. My Harold been gone for about ten years, and I have no reason to look any further into that hole. But I would like to keep that cold air out. I never thought about there being a tunnel down there, A mine shaft makes better sense to me. Some shafts are pretty close to the surface. You want to look in my basement?" They said yes, together.

She led them around to the back of the house, then thru a back door leading into a small old kitchen, and straight ahead was another door. That door opened to the basement, and they could feel the damp cold right away. She carefully led the way down narrow steps and pulled on a string hanging from a single light bulb that bathed the basement in dim light. It was damp and musty smelling down there in the semi-darkness. Some old furniture was piled in one corner, along with shelves that held a variety of old toys, gardening equipment and miscellaneous junk. She pointed to the shelves and said "My husband patched up that wall behind those shelves as best he could, but the cold air still comes thru. If you put your hand against the wall, you'll feel the cold air. Move your hand around and you'll see. Dan and Bruce both felt the wall, with was very cool. Bruce moved his hand around and said "I feel the cold air. What do you think, Dan?"

Dan felt it, too. He turned to the old lady, who now had a shawl wrapped around her. "If we removed some of these concrete blocks to see if there really is a hole leading to a tunnel or something, when we're done, I would patch up the hole for you and you won't feel any more cold air. It would sure save us a lot of time and sweat from digging a hole into that hill side. If that's ok with you."

She agreed, and they said they would return in a day or two with proper equipment for digging and cave exploring. They exchanged names and phone numbers, then Dan and Bruce and Bennie drove home.

Chapter Nineteen

Bruce offered the use of his pickup truck and some of his tools for the digging operation. They met the next morning at McDonalds. Dan had offered to let old Bennie ride with them again, but he declined, saying he'd rather hear about it after all the hard work was done.

The elderly homeowner appeared to be wearing the same housedress as she greeted them at the door. She eyed the tools in the back of the truck and said, "You aren't gonna tear up my basement too much are you?"

They assured her they wouldn't, and would repair any damage, as they said yesterday. Bruce handed Dan a pick and a coil of rope. He hefted a couple of shovels and they descended into the basement. Before they could do anything, they unloaded some shelving, then with a screech, scooted the heavy board shelves away from the cold wall. Bruce motioned to Dan to stand back, then swung the heavy sledge hammer hard against the wall. A few splinters of concrete fell away. He tried once more, then handed the big hammer to Dan, "Your turn."

Dan swung the hammer. Again and again, the concrete held fast. "Her husband mixed up some good concrete here. I probably would have destroyed my basement by now." He swung the big hammer again, this time making a small hole in the wall. "Hey, we're getting somewhere." Dan aimed his flashlight thru the hole. All he could see was blackness, but was greeted by more cold air. He took the sledge hammer from Bruce and wacked the wall several more times, each time creating a bigger hole. After nearly an hour, they had a hole six inches in diameter.

"You know," said Dan, "If this were a TV show, this hole would have been large enough to walk thru by now." Just then, someone started down the steps. It was the young police chief. "You guys making any progress?" They showed him the hole. "Her husband made some pretty hard concrete here. It's been slow going," said Bruce. Dan handed the chief his flashlight so he could look thru the hole.

"I don't see anything," he said.

"We're not done yet," said Dan. "You're always welcome to stay and help."

"Well, I would love to help you guys," he said, "but I need to make my rounds, you know. Besides, I might get dirty." They laughed. "Holler if you find something," he said as he headed back up the steps.

They enlarged the hole considerably in the next two hours, then decided to take a break for lunch. At the convenience store again, they were met with questions from some of the townsfolk who had quickly heard about their digging. One man, with fly a flyaway haircut, and a huge stomach outfitted in sagging bib overhauls, wanted to know if they were opening up an old coal mine. "I been looking for work, but there's not much work to be had around here, you know." Dan thought to himself the man probably wasn't looking too hard, judging from his physique.

Back at the house, they took turns pounding the wall, making the hole slightly larger with each passing hour. By four o'clock, they had a hole nearly large enough to climb thru. They decided to stop for the day.

*   *   *   *   *

On the way home, Dan's cell phone chirped. It was Elizabeth. She rarely called from the hospital.

"Dan, I need your help!" She sounded out of breath. "The boys were on a school field trip at Giant City State Park, and Mikey is missing. Somehow he got separated from the rest of the group. I'm on my way there now. They're organizing a search party to search the woods. Could you fly over there in your little plane and see if you can spot him? Please?" Dan said he would leave right away for the airstrip. He stopped long enough to fill up two gas cans and raced out to the airstrip northeast of town. He pulled the Quicksilver ultralight out of the hangar, dumped the fuel in, and fired up the engine. After a quick check of his instruments and insuring the controls were free, he pointed the nose down the runway and pushed the throttle to the stops. He climbed out in a hard left bank and headed towards the most beautiful, if not the most rugged state park in Illinois. Giant City was a favorite of rock climbers and rapellers. With darkness only a couple of hours away, there was no time to waste. Top speed on the little ultralight was nothing like larger general aviation airplanes, but he pushed it as fast as he dared without overheating the engine. If the two stroke engine locked up because of overheating, it would do nobody any good, especially if he were still in the air. Then they would be looking for him, as well. The flight from his airstrip to the state park seemed to take forever, with the ground slowly rolling past underneath. As he got closer, he spotted the winking red and blue lights of police cars thru the trees as well as search and rescue trucks. He circled the lodge, then cut the engine and dropped into a not too graceful landing right in the parking lot, between the trees and light poles. A cop ran towards him, waving his arms. "Hey, are you nuts? You could have been killed! What are you doing here?" yelled the young cop. "My girlfriend called me. It's her little boy that's missing. I'm going to help find him." "The hell you are," said the cop, scowling at Dan. You're going to stay on the ground, and we're going to impound that there airplane, because you made an unauthorized landing on state property. So get off that thing and show me some ID." Just then, Elizabeth ran up to Dan and flung her arms around him. "Oh, I'm so glad you could come. This just isn't like Mikey. We've been out here several times before and he never did anything like this. But this is the first time he was with his school class and not with Mason and me." Her eyes were red from crying. "Well, according to this cop, I'm grounded. He won't let me join the searchers." What?" Elizabeth whirled around to face the cop. The cop put on his most stern face. "This guy had no right to land here. I'm placing him under arrest for trespassing on state property." Another, older cop, a state trooper, walked over and listened as the younger officer was talking to Elizabeth. "I saw you land that Quicksilver. Pretty good landing, I must say, considering where you had to put her down." He stuck out his hand to Dan. "My name's Marvin Williston. I also have a Quicksilver, but I'm not sure I could have landed here without rolling it up into a pile of tubing. You seem like a pretty good pilot." Dan said, "Thanks. This officer won't let me search for her little boy." The state cop motioned for the other younger cop to follow him off a short distance. They had an animated conversation for a moment, then the younger cop, threw up his hands and stalked off.

The state cop returned to Dan and Elizabeth. "If you think you can get off outta here ok, I suggest you get airborne and start looking before we run out of daylight. OK?" Dan, Elizabeth and the state cop talked for a couple of minutes more, with Elizabeth giving directions where the school kids were when Mikey wandered off. Dan picked up the tail of the ultralight and swung it around and set it down. Then he motioned for everyone to stand back as he settled into the pilot's seat and strapped in. One quick look around, he yelled "clear!" and started the motor. The little Rotax two stroke motor screamed as he fed it full throttle and raced across the parking lot. He easily lifted off and banked over the trees towards the ravine where Mikey was last seen.

Mikey had his hands full, trying to hold the squirming little puppy still as he climbed the hillside as best he could and keep his balance. He stumbled several times, but he was determined to hold onto the little puppy. He had noticed it thru the trees and brush while his class was hiking thru the forest in the big state park. He had been there before with his mom and Mason, on picnics, and he thought he knew where he was in the woods, but now he wasn't so sure. He hadn't seen anyone else so he didn't call out. The woods thinned out and he found himself on the edge of a big field filled with big round hay bales. The puppy squirmed again, and tickled him with it's tongue just then, and he giggled. A noise overhead made him stop and listen. It sounded like an airplane. He listened as it grew louder, then passed right overhead. It was Dan!

He ran the way the ultralight went, hoping to see it again. Holding the puppy made running difficult.

Dan soared over the forest just a few feet above the trees. It was nearly impossible see thru the canopy, but he tried. Several times he caught himself looking down and the little plane flew closer to the trees then he liked. Dipping the wheels into tree branches would spell instant trouble, so he gave himself a little more altitude. A field grew out of the forest, covered with round hay bales. Elizabeth liked to call them 'tootsie Rolls for cows'. That made Dan chuckle. The boys picked up on it too, and when they drove by a field of hay bales, somebody would yell out, "There's a tootsie roll field!"

He decided that the field would be about as far as Mikey could have gotten, as a creek would its way thru the forest on the far side of the field. He swung around in a lazy arc, and prepared to fly another leg back towards the lodge. Something caught his eye off to the right. It was Mikey, running across the field and waving with one arm. Dan pulled the nose up to slow down and loose altitude, then steered the Quicksilver down to the ground towards Mikey. The freshly cut hay field made for a soft landing. He saw what Mikey was carrying, then he looked past Mikey at something else that caught his eye. It was a mother Coyote, head down, racing towards them. "Mikey, put the coyote down!" yelled Dan. "No! It's a little puppy!" said Mikey, "He's mine. I found him."

Dan said, "Mikey, You found a wild animal. And his mother wants him back. Now put-the-puppy-down-Now!" Mikey had made it to the ultralight, still half carrying, half dragging the coyote puppy. He had a defiant look on his face. "Mikey, here comes his mother and she'll hurt you!" yelled Dan, over the noise of the engine. Mikey turned around and saw the mother coyote just a few feet away, head down, baring her fangs. Suddenly, Mikey let go of the puppy and scrambled into the passenger seat of the ultralight and at the same time, Dan shoved the throttle forward all the way. The Quicksilver nearly ran into a hay bale before Dan could steer around it. The field was like a jigsaw puzzle as Dan wound his way around bale after bale, looking for an opening large enough to take off in. At the edge of the field, he felt he had enough room, and gave it full throttle. They leaped off the ground just as the airplane kissed a nearby hay bale with the wheels.

Dan breathed a sigh of relief as they flew over the lodge. He circled the lodge twice to show everybody on the ground that he had found Mikey. He could pick out Elizabeth and Mason who were waving back at them. Then he waggled his wings and he and Mikey flew back to his airstrip. It was almost dark as he lightly touched down. He taxied the ultralight to his barn hanger and shut off the motor. The silence enveloped them as Mikey struggled to help Dan push the airplane inside. After they had piled into the Jeep, Dan headed for Elizabeth's house. As they pulled into the drive, Dan noticed that Mikey was fast asleep. Elizabeth and Mason weren't home from Giant City State Park yet, so he gently carried the boy up the front steps and sat down on the porch swing, with Mikey's head in his lap. When Elizabeth and Mason drove home later, she found both of them asleep in the porch swing.

* * * * *

Dan and his rescue of Mikey from coyotes' made the front page of the Carbondale newspaper. At least they got their story straight. The local TV station's reporter had a breathless account of him fighting off a pack of wolves as he took off.

His mother refilled his coffee cup at breakfast. As he read the paper, his cell phone chirped. Another text message from his boss in Chicago. After breakfast, he did a little work around his mother's house, then returned the call after office hours began.

After exchanging greetings, his boss said, "Got another one for you, Dan." "What do you have for me this time, Gregg?" "Got a fella down in Tennessee who has an Aviat Husky. He's into us for about two hundred thousand dollars. He stopped his payments about three months ago, and now he won't take our calls at his office. Our registered letters have fallen on deaf ears. So, it's time to take his toy away from him. I'll send you all the paperwork via FEDEX and you can take it from there, ok?"

"Ok. Wish me luck." Dan hung up. He sent a text to CJ Rodriguez to be ready to meet up at the Marion airport in a couple of days and take on another repo job. CJ sent back an immediate text saying he was packing his bag and would leave right away. Dan spent the day cleaning out gutters and installing covers on them to keep out leaves and debris. By the end of the day, he still wasn't done, but he'd made a good start. At least there was no rain in the forecast for a few days.

Chapter Twenty

After CJ called Dan while waiting for his connecting flight out of St Louis, Dan met him at the Marion airport. It seemed to Dan that the short squat little Cuban was happiest when he was causing some confusion or making mischief somewhere. CJ was always underestimated by people who didn't know him, and he wanted it that way. Dan always said that nobody would see CJ in a crowd of three. Like Dan, he could fly just about anything with wings or rotor blades; in addition he could take them apart and rebuild them too, which made him handy to have around in case there was no key available to start an airplane, or if they needed to disable an airplane by stealing the prop. For this trip, Dan and CJ decided that Dan would play the part of a bank manager, dressed up in a suit and tie, hoping to take possession of the Aviat Husky airplane simply and easily. First, he left CJ sitting in the rental car at the airport, while Dan approached the airport manager about returning the airplane. The airport manager was a mousy little man, with thinning hair, wearing what appeared to be off the rack clothing in various shades of brown and tan, probably from JC Penny. After a cordial enough introduction, the airport manager coughed nervously, then asked Dan to wait outside his office in the airport lobby for a few minutes.

Dan was looking at for sale ads and posters on a bulletin board near the manager's office when two policemen strode into the lobby, looked around and came over to Dan.

"Are you Mr Flatt?" the older of the two asked. Dan stood up quickly, stuck out his hand, and said "Yes, that's me." Neither cop offered to shake hands. They just stared at Dan for a moment.

Finally, the older cop handed Dan back his paperwork and said, "The paperwork you brought with you isn't valid in this county. I'm afraid you're not going to be able to repossess anything without going thru my office first. You understand?"

Dan said, "Our legal department gave me this paperwork. Everything's in order, legally. The owner is behind in his payments, and my bank wants this plane back."

"The owner of that airplane is a fine upstanding citizen of this county. I've personally known him a long time. And that man employs a lot of people around here in several businesses, and he pays a lot of taxes. So, it doesn't matter what you or your bank wants, you're not going to get anything from this man. I don't want to seem unfriendly, but you're not welcome here anymore." He gave Dan a stern look. "I think you should be careful not to break any speed laws as you leave this county. And, you should leave now. We clear on that?" Dan nodded his head slowly, as if it just dawned on him that he was not going to accomplish anything more today. With that, the cops turned around and left the airport office.

Dan waited a moment while the cops left the parking lot, then walked outside only to find his car missing. He broke into a smile as CJ came tooling back up the airport road. He motioned for CJ to swing by and pick him up. He filled him in on what the cops said. CJ nodded his head.

'When the cops arrived, I decided to head out. I drove down the road a ways to a convenience store and waited for them to return. When they drove by, I came back. They're really friendly around here, huh?"

Dan said, "Looks like it."

CJ grinned. "I was gong to slash all four of their tires, but that would have looked suspicious, don't you think?" They both chuckled at that.

CJ drove across the county line, careful not to arouse attention of the county police car that followed them several cars back. "Glad this is a rental," said Dan. They might be watching for this car in the future." CJ turned to look at Dan. "You have a plan B?" Dan just smiled. "I'll tell you all about it over dinner tonight. Elizabeth invited me over for steaks cooked on the grill. I think I'm doing the cooking and I'm also bringing the steaks. So, I'll just pick up an extra steak. It'll be a good time to introduce you to her. She's quite a gal." They drove the next few hours in near silence. Dan was lost in his thoughts, and CJ did what he does best...he slept.

Elizabeth was delighted to meet CJ and the boys thought he was a riot as he regaled them with his 'adventures' while growing up in old Cuba.

Later, while Elizabeth was getting the boys ready for bed, Dan said to CJ "I saw a poster for an airshow at the airport we were at, coming up next weekend. We might be able to recover the Husky during the airshow." He outlined his plan and CJ's smile grew wider. If we pull this off, Amigo, we could make a 'made-For-TV'" movie out of it! Sounds like something Burt Reynolds and Dom Delouise would have tried." They both laughed at that.

Elizabeth came out of the house and sat down in a lawn chair next to Dan. CJ stood up and stretched. "Elizabeth, you are a gracious hostess, and your two boys are well behaved. And you, sir," he turned to Dan and bowed from the waist, "You cook a mean steak. With that, I will say Adios. I will await your call, Daniel."

They watched as CJ left in his rental car. "He's going back to LA tonight?" said Elizabeth.

"If I know CJ, he'll probably pick up some unsuspecting stewardess near St Louis, and tomorrow, at the crack of dawn, he'll be on a flight back to home. He flies more than anybody I know. He loves it. Gives him a chance to meet people, he says." A few minutes later, Dan said his goodbyes and headed home. He was planning to tackle more projects around his mother's house tomorrow.

Chapter Twenty-One

The airshow was typical of many airshows held across the country every summer. People came from miles around to the carnival-like atmosphere created by blending pilots who were showing off their airplanes, many of which were home built. Today, nearly two hundred brightly colored airplanes lined the runways. Crowds milled about the airplanes as pilots answered questions, with some giving rides to kids as their parents watched nervously from the ground. A couple of antique car clubs were present, with their perfectly restored automobiles from decades past gleaming brightly in the summer sun. Skydivers floated gently towards earth in the slight breeze, as an announcer outlined the events coming up during the afternoon. Ice cream sellers, along with cotton candy and hot dogs were present everywhere.

One act that was not announced but on the schedule was where a pilot posing as a drunk farmer complete in bib overalls and straw hat would wander among the airplanes, and make his way towards a bright yellow Piper Cub that had just been started. While the "pilot" was busy untying the plane, the drunk would stumble into the cockpit and gun the motor, causing the plane to suddenly take rush down between the rows of aircraft and take off. The plane would flop down on the ground again, rise up into the air, flop down to the ground again, then make a sharp turn back toward the "pilot" and police who were now running after the airplane, only to be running for their lives as the plane dove towards them. Great fun for the crowd. If they only knew how many hours of planning had gone into polishing the drunk act, and how many times that same airplane had been "stolen" at airshows across the country, the crowds would be amazed. Today, however, there would be a slight twist.

As Dan and CJ had hoped for, the airplane they needed to repossess was present among the dozens of little airplanes lined up along the flightline. To make things a little easier, this time they had a duplicate key for the door which also fit the ignition, one provided by the bank and kept in reserve with the paperwork, in case of a loan that had to be recalled.

This particular airplane was yellow, with blue trim, much like the Cub that would be used in the drunk farmer act. The owner had flown the plane that morning and parked it among the others so he could show it off to his friends and other aircraft owners. They then wandered off to enjoy the airshow. Dan ID'd the pilot/owner of the Husky from a photo he had in his pocket. He wanted to make sure the owner was plenty far away when his airplane was to be repo'd. The owner and his daughter were talking to friends over by some food vendors on the opposite side of the grandstands.

Dan and CJ sauntered among the airplanes, keeping an eye on the one they wanted. Dan even wandered over to the plane and peered into the window, and at the same time unlocking the door, shielding his actions with his body. Then he wandered off. Soon the airshow would begin.

CJ commandeered an unused golf cart and picked up Dan. They watched from nearby where the crowds were assembled in bleacher seating as the National anthem was played while two skydivers descended to earth with a giant American flag unfurled beneath their feet. Then the airshow began. Several airshow acts were performing or ready to perform. The crowd applauded while a small plane did corkscrew maneuvers while trailing a thick cloud of smoke.

CJ noticed the drunken pilot act was about to begin, so he and Dan took off in the golf cart and drove thru the parked airplanes. After a quick glance around, he dropped Dan off at the repo plane. He then drove around the plane and stopped to untie the left wing and then the tail, while Dan untied the right wing. After that, he then propped open the upper part of the door against the bottom of the wing, and dropped the bottom half of the door against the fuselage. After lightly jumping into the pilot's seat, he switched on the ignition, yelled "Clear!" and the prop swung into a silver blur. A quick check of the controls and he opened the throttle and the plane began to move. He made sure the area between the rows of planes was clear, then pushed the throttle completely to the stop, which sent the little plane surging ahead. In only a couple hundred feet, the plane was airborne, and Dan kept the plane just ten feet off the ground as he raced past the end of the rows of planes.

Meanwhile, the real drunk pilot act had begun, with the other yellow Cub already in the air and turning back towards its pursuers, while the crowd howled with delight. A young teenage girl looked past the drunken pilot act and said to her father, "That looks a lot like our plane over there." Her father was laughing and talking with someone sitting next to him, and it took him a moment to react to what his daughter had just said. When she pointed out the plane that was nearly out of sight at the other end of the airfield, he patted her knee, and said "Yep, it does look a lot like our plane." Then he looked down the rows of planes and it took him a few seconds to understand what he was not seeing. He was not seeing his airplane. There was a hole in the line of airplanes, one where his plane had been. He jumped up, pushing past others who were watching the drunken pilot act and yelled towards a local cop who was watching nearby. The cop thought he was a part of the act and just grinned, thumbs hooked in his belt. By the time he made the cop understand what had just happened, the plane was out of sight. It was hard to hear, between the roar of the airplanes circling overhead and the cheers from the crowd as they hooted and hollered for the drunken farmer and the hapless cops chasing after him.

Dan Flatt dug a handheld GPS unit out of his pocket and turned it on. Once he had his home airport pulled up, he set the GPS on top of the instrument panel and settled down. He had several hundred miles to go, flying at tree top level in order to stay under any FAA radar that might be looking for him. He wasn't worried about the FAA, but if alerted, local cops might be advised to shoot first and ask questions later. He and CJ had planned a rendezvous at an airport just over the state line in Kentucky, out of the jurisdiction of the local Tennessee cops, about fifty miles from where Dan "stole" the plane.

The Kentucky airport came up over the horizon and Dan made a gentle landing in the little plane. He taxied over to the fuel pumps and shut down. A line boy came out of the office and started the gas pump, while pulling a ladder over to the front of the wing. In fifteen minutes, both wing tanks were filled and Dan was careful to pay in cash and got a receipt. That way a credit card couldn't be traced.

"Where you headed? " asked the line boy casually.

"Back to Missouri," Dan said. "Oh," said the line boy. He seemed a little nervous. Dan picked up on the nervousness and decided to leave promptly.

"Sure you don't want to borrow the courtesy car and go into town and get something to eat?"

Dan smiled. "Thanks, but I need to head on home. My wife will be wondering where I am." He pocketed the gas receipt and headed out the door. He had planned on waiting for CJ but instinct told him he should leave right away.

He settled himself into the pilot's seat once again and fired up the little Continental engine. After checking the gauges, he taxied out to the runway and turned into the wind. He pushed the throttle to the firewall easily and the little plane nearly jumped into the air. As he cleared the airport, he saw CJ pulling into the parking lot. He knew CJ would be wondering what was going on, and he started to make a low pass to alert CJ that he might be in trouble, when a police car raced into the parking lot. Dan yelled at CJ on his cell phone and told him to just keep driving, and he would see him at the Marion airport later. Dan flew the rest of the way home at just above the treetops, in order to stay off FAA radar. The little portable GPS he had perched on top of the instrument panel, let him fly cross country direct to Marion, IL.

That evening, with the airplane safely inside a locked hangar at the Marion airport, Dan waited until CJ's car was in Elizabeth's driveway before starting the pork chops on the grill. Over a well-earnd beer later, they laughed as they recounted each other's tales of "stealing" the airplane.

CJ said, "You should have seen the look on that drunk farmer's face when we stole his show. Nobody was hearing a word of it. They all thought he was a part of the act and they just played along. It wasn't until the owner of your plane grabbed the sheriff that they realized they'd been had. Then all hell broke loose. I nearly got run over by a cop car as they tried to keep you in sight. Lucky for us they didn't have any faster airplanes handy. By the time they could scramble one, you were nowhere to be found."

Dan sent a text message to the bank in Chicago that the plane was theirs again, then went to bed.

Chapter Twenty-Two

The next morning, Dan opened the door to his hangar out in the country. He pulled the sheet from the wings and put it on the workbench next to the wall. Then he stood on a stepstool and checked the gas in the wing tank. It was full. By keeping the tank full, it eliminated condensation which would add water to the gas. Enough water and the gas would choke and possible stall the engine. Keeping the gas tank full was important. Then he checked all the cables and lines running from the wings to the tail and back. A friend of his had forgotten to check everything before he went flying, or he would have noticed that a bolt had worked itself loose from the tail. During his flight, the bolt came all the way loose and cause the tail to flutter, and the ultralight became uncontrollable. He crashed and spent months in the hospital and rehab. All because he forgot to stick to his checklist. Dan never forgot that lesson from his friend. He pulled the little plane from its hangar/barn and settled himself into his seat. After strapping himself in, he turned on the gas, and flipped on the master switch. After looking around to make sure nobody was near, he yelled "Clear!" and pushed the starter button. The little two stroke engine roared into life and at once tried to move the plane. Dan held fast to the brakes as he tested the throttle. Then he moved all the controls to make sure everything worked the way they were supposed to. Only then did he put on his headset to drown out the engine noise. He released the brakes and taxied to the end of the runway. Nobody had ever landed at his little airstrip, and he wasn't sure anybody else knew about it but he always practiced good pilotage and before takeoff, he did a 360 degree turn at the end of the runway to insure that nobody was about to land as he took off. He completed his turn, pointed the plane down the runway and released the brakes while opening the throttle. The plane surged ahead and nearly leaped into the air, as if it couldn't wait to be airborne. The ground fell away, the trees got smaller and with every foot of altitude he could see further and further. The lush greenery of Southern Illinois unfolded as he climbed into the sky and headed towards Herrin.

Not having a radio, he made sure to avoid the Marion airport by a wide margin and by staying low. He certainly didn't want to tangle with an incoming private jet, which would be upon him before he could get out of the way. Forty miles per hour was no match for one hundred and thirty, which was the landing speed of some jets. But, he reckoned, at forty miles per hour, you could see things much more clearly than at 130. Their loss, he mused. They're all business in those jets, while I'm out here having the time of my life. He flew on.

The railroad tracks led from downtown Herrin straight east, then began to angle in a more southerly direction towards Marion. At one point, you could see where tracks used to run, because the trees lined what used to be the trackbed. No tracks were present now. He followed one trackbed for a while until it turned north towards the little town of Pittsburg, east of Marion. Then they abruptly stopped in a field. So he turned around and flew back to the last set of tracks. The day was sunny with little white puffy clouds, a perfect day for flying. He passed several houses where women were hanging washing out on the lines. They waved at him and he waved back.

*   *   *   *   *

Junior Gulledge watched as the driver from Missouri backed up the semi trailer towards the barn. Peanut was directing him. He held up his hands to stop, then they opened up the back of the trailer. The driver hopped down from the cab of the truck and helped them open up the trailer. This trailer was equipped with a hydraulic loading platform that unfolded from below the trailer to make a 6x 8 foot level loading platform that could be raised and lowered from the ground to the level of the trailer. This made loading much faster and easier. Nothing had to be pushed up a ramp anymore. They were nearly half done loading before they heard the ultralight. The wind was from the south, and it approached from the north so it was nearly on top of them before they heard it. By then it was too late to hide anything.

Junior heard it first. He craned his neck then saw it flash above the trees overhead. "It's him again!" said Junior. "He found us! Were in trouble now!"

The driver of the semi scooted around the truck to the cab and pulled out a shotgun. Then he strode to a clear spot in the trees and waited for the ultralight to complete its turn. When it was right overhead, he let go with three shots in a row. They watched as the little plane bucked when hit then angled off towards the east. Presently they heard the motor stop. The driver said, "Well if I didn't kill him, he's hurtin' bad. I recon he'll pile 'er up somewhere. By the time he gets found, we'll be long gone." Junior just stared at the driver, who nonchalantly had just shot someone. He let out an involuntary shiver. Then he decided he should keep busy. In less than thirty minutes they had the truck packed. The driver paid them all handsomely, and drove off. Junior and Peanut and Wayman looked at each other.

Peanut said, "Boys we had a good haul. We've been paid. I think we should call it quits for quite a while before our luck takes a turn for the worse. As far as that airplane goes, we didn't see nothin. OK?" They agreed on that. They piled into Peanuts truck and drove home

From the air, Dan saw the farmhouse with the mowers, four wheelers and other assorted stolen power items about the same time as they saw him. First a flash thru the trees then he was on top of the farmhouse. At treetop level he could pick out about thirty items about to be loaded into the back of a semi. As he passed overhead, He looked around him to make a mental note of his location, then made a sweeping turn back over the house and barn. He never heard the shotgun over the roar of his engine, but something like a baseball bat hit him in the ribs. A second later he was slapped on the side of the head hard, and nearly passed out. He felt his cheek and came away with blood, and instantly realized he had been hit with something. It didn't dawn on him that it was buckshot from a shotgun, because at the same time, he had a terrible headache and his vision blurred. To make matters worse, his engine stopped. The silence really got his attention, because from the treetops, he had only a few seconds to decide what to do. His vision was swimming in and out of focus, so he steered straight ahead and aimed for a grassy field. As he swooped down to the grass, a large oak tree grew up in front of him so he mashed the rudder pedal to the left just as the plane touched down at the base of the tree. The wing smacked the tree and flipped the little plane around, throwing Dan clear. He rolled over a couple of times coming to rest face down in the grass.

Dan Flatt never considered himself a lucky man. He just never thought about it. Today, his guardian angel was riding on his shoulder. He was in good shape, he was young and healthy. And, one field over, a twelve year old Mennonite boy was herding several young steers towards their barn, when he heard the faint boom of a shotgun, then saw the plane lose altitude and disappear behind the trees. He jumped the fence, then ran across the field to Dan, who was unconscious and covered in blood. The boy knelt beside Dan, unsure about what to do for him. At first the boy thought Dan was dead, but his eyelids fluttered, startling the youngster, who then ran home, summoned his parents and led them to Dan. They immediately began to administer first aid, and they used Dan's cellphone, which they found in his pocket, to call police and an ambulance. He was rushed to a hospital in Marion where he was put in intensive care. His driver's license held a Chicago address, and nothing on him said anything about him being from Carterville or about Elizabeth and her boys. So when the police inquired about his Chicago address, nobody answered to confirm or deny where he lived.

That evening, Elizabeth wondered where Dan was. He hadn't called, which was unusual. He always called each evening if just to say hi. Finally, she couldn't stand it any longer, so she called his cell phone. A strange voice answered. "Hello?"

"I'm calling Dan Flatt. Who is this?"

"This is Sargent Oliver Smith with the Williamson County Sheriff's Dept. Who is THIS?"

"Dan Flatt is my boyfriend, er friend. He always calls me each day. He hasn't called. I wanted to check up on him. Is he in jail?"

The sergeant nearly cleared his throat, "No Ma'am. He's in the hospital. At Marion. In intensive care."

"What?! What happened?"

"Someone shot him down in his little airplane, is what happened," the deputy said. "Lucky for him a young Mennonite boy was nearby and heard and saw him go down. Otherwise we might never have found him before it was too late."

"He's at the Marion Hospital?"

"Yes Ma'am." Elizabeth hung up and started to grab her car keys. Then she had another thought. She looked up Dan's mother's number and called her. She knew she would want to go to the hospital, too, so she offered to swing by and pick her up. They rode over together. The boys sat quietly in the back seat. Elizabeth told them they were too young to go see Dan, and they might have to stay in the waiting room. For once, the boys, were ok with that.

When the nurse admitted them into Dan's room, Elizabeth took in all the white sheets, bandages, and IV's that seemed to go everywhere. The side of Dan's face was covered with bandages; his arm was strapped to his side and he was asleep. His mother put her hand to her mouth and Elizabeth thought she was going to scream when she saw Dan, but she didn't. Elizabeth moved herself near his mother's side in case she fainted or something. His mother stood next to Dan's bed and put out her hand as if to touch him, but didn't. She turned to Elizabeth, "I want to touch my boy so badly but I'm afraid I'll only hurt him worse. I don't know what to do!"

They leaned on each other for support. The tears flowed. Then they hugged each other and moved out into the hall. "Who would do such a thing to my boy?" said his mother.

Elizabeth said, "I don't know but I hope the police will find him. Or them. I'd like to be there when they do."

Elizabeth learned thru the sheriff's department that Dan's ultralight had been moved from the farm field to an impound lot at the Sheriff's dept. At least there, it would be safe. The engine had quit because some buckshot severed the fuel line, causing raw fuel to be dumped overboard instead of into the engine. When the plane hit the tree, it knocked a wing completely off as it spun the plane around. The way the ultralight was made, the aluminum structure absorbed much of the impact, and actually saved Dan's life by crushing some of the components first before getting to him.

Chapter Twenty-Three

When Elizabeth left the hospital with her boys and Dan's mom, she was filled with different emotions. She was glad Dan was going to be OK, she was worried for his mother, and she was really upset that somebody would try to kill him. She decided to pay a visit to the Sheriff later that day and try to find out more about what happened.

Later that day, she sat across from the Sheriff in his office, and listened as he and a detective filled her in on what they knew. The deputies had searched the area and had found no clues as to why somebody would take a shot at an airplane. They had visited the old farmstead and found lots of tracks made by four wheelers, mowers, and tractors, all running over each other, as well as tire tracks made by a much larger vehicle, such as a semi tractor trailer. "Any idea why somebody would try to shoot at him?" asked the Sheriff. "He have any enemies that you know of?" Both the sheriff and the detective listened close as she gathered her thoughts. "Yes and no. Last week, somebody stole my John Deere garden tractor. I had some rust spots on the hood and I didn't have any green paint, so I used some pink spray paint I found in my garage." The two men looked at each other when she said 'pink'. "I know it didn't look very nice, but John Deere charges an arm and a leg for their paint and this was handy, so..." "Anyway, we were flying the day before yesterday in the afternoon in his ultralight airplane and flew over an old farm, and I thought I saw my garden tractor down there on the ground. It was with a bunch of other stuff, like mowers and motorcycles and stuff."

She continued: "When we got back on the ground, Dan found the farm on Google Earth and we drove out there. The place had been cleaned out. We even met the old guy that owned the farm and talked to him. He had rented it to some guys for several months. Guys who paid cash. And, one of your deputies drove up while we were there, too. He didn't find anything either, so he left. Last night, Dan wondered if we had spooked the guys and they hid everything. Because he must have seen something today or they wouldn't have shot at him."

The sheriff said, "Could you point out the farm on Google Earth?" She said she could. They brought up Google Earth on the desktop computer and she quickly identified the farm. The sheriff stabbed his intercom and said, "Get Grady on the radio and ask him to check the old Martin farm again, off of Winchester Road."

The sheriff said they had had complaints from people all over the county who were having items stolen from their yards and farms. They also had complaints from Saline county, as well. A couple of minutes later the clerk called back. "Grady said he did, and the place was abandoned, but he also said someone had been there recently because there were a lot of tire tracks."

Elizabeth said, "Somebody broke into my house in Carterville last week." The sheriff and the detective looked at each other. "What? Tell us about it." "Well, a neighbor saw a guy go into my basement, and called the Carterville police. They got him when he came out of my house. He didn't have anything on him. But the next night, my garden tractor went missing. Now that I think of it, maybe he's involved someway. He works at the nursing home, he's an orderly. At least, I think he still works there." She decided not to say anything about the money in her basement. "Probably would be a good idea to stay away from him." He looked at his detective. "Wouldn't hurt to have a talk with him," said the sheriff. "I'll give Carterville a call." As she got up to leave, the sheriff said "Oh, by the way. We got a call from the FAA. Shooting at an airplane of any kind makes it a federal offense. So now it's a federal crime, in addition to a state and local one. If we catch these guys, they're going to go to prison for awhile." The sheriff stood up and said, "Elizabeth, I'm just glad you weren't flying around with your boyfriend when he got shot. It might have been you there in the hospital with him, or worse." She shivered at the thought of somebody angry enough to shoot at her.

Junior couldn't sleep that night. His mind kept seeing the casual way the driver of that semi had pulled the shotgun out of the truck and shot down that airplane, as if it was no big deal. Little had been said after that. Then the boys had loaded the truck as quickly as they could and watched silently as the truck left the farm. That dream played itself out over and over all night. The next morning, Junior went to work at the nursing home, glad to not be stealing things ever again. He even said "Good morning," to the director who gave him a curt nod and walked off, only to turn around a moment later when she realized who it was that had just been nice to her.

Chapter Twenty-Four

Dan spent two more days in the hospital before the doctors would let him go home. He was anxious to be out of the hospital and doing anything other than laying in a hospital bed. Even the nurses weren't enough to make him want to stay. Especially with a good looking nurse who would look over him at home.

Elizabeth and his mother showed up at check out time, along with Mikey and Mason. He was happy to see them all as they wheeled him out to Elizabeth's car. He was all grins as he prepared to stand up from the wheelchair, when the pain hit him in the lower back. He nearly fell over, and had to suppress a gasp as he turned around and sat back in the front seat. Luckily, no one seemed to notice, and they pulled away from the hospital and drove home to his mother's house. He spent the rest of the day in bed, sleeping with aid of some pills he'd been given.

The next morning, he rolled over gingerly in bed and slowly sat up. 'So this is what it feels to be a hundred years old' he thought as all the aches and pains wracked his body. He managed to stand up and hobbled to the bathroom. After cleaning up, he slowly descended the stairs from his bedroom to the kitchen. His mother was busy doing something in the kitchen, but stopped and watched him closely as he leaned on the side of the stove on his way to the table. When he sat down at the table, his back screamed briefly. She watched him closely, but said nothing. He decided he would stay sitting down for a while, right there. After the breakfast dishes were washed, and he had drained two cups of coffee, his mother pulled out a chair and sat down next to him. She put her hand on his arm and squeezed slightly. "This must be the only part of you that doesn't hurt," she said. His look back at her said it all. "Yeah, mom, I feel like I've been beat up."

"Who would do such a thing?" she said.

"Well, I saw a bunch of stuff on the ground at one of the little farms I flew over. I really don't remember much about anything right now. Maybe it'll come back to me, or I'll remember something else."

She said "I've heard that when you have an accident, you sort of blank out the whole thing, and might not ever remember anything about it, ever." He smiled a weak smile at her and she got up and put her arms around him as he sat at the table and let out a small sob. "You'll be all right, I just know you will," she said.

Chapter Twenty-Five

He healed slowly over the next two weeks. Elizabeth brought the boys over to his mom's house several times, and each time he played with them a little more. And each morning after they had visited, he felt a little less like he'd been run over, and like a little more of his old self.

Finally, one morning, he announced to his mother that he was going to rent a trailer and bring what was left of his ultralight airplane home from the police impound yard.

At his little grass airstrip, he backed up the trailer to the barn he used for a hangar, and untied the plane. It took him two hours to get all the parts off the trailer and into the hangar. He spread out the pieces and started an inventory of what was broken or bent and what could be reused. Surprisingly enough, his list was not as long as he figured it would be. He was using the back of an envelope to write down what he thought he needed. The sound of a car approaching made him stop.

Elizabeth and the two boys piled out of her Camry with a picnic lunch. They spread a blanket on the ground beside the hangar, under the shade of a huge oak tree. It was time for him to take a break, and just having Elizabeth and the boys nearby made him feel better. He made a phone call to an ultralight dealer near Evansville, Indiana and placed his order. Everything was in stock, so he asked Elizabeth if they would all like to ride to Indiana with him. The boys yelled YES! But Elizabeth declined, saying she had lots of chores to do and it would be nice to have the boys gone for a few hours so she could have some time to herself. After strapping the boys in, he gassed up the Jeep and drove out of Carterville, thru Harrisburg, to Mt Vernon, Indiana. The sun was a half hour from setting when he returned the trailer after unloading the parts, and returning the boys. He ate a light supper at his mom's, then settled down in his dad's easy chair in front of the TV. Around midnight, he woke up to find a blanket draped over his body and the TV turned off. He climbed the stairs to his bedroom and went to bed.

The next several days went by in a blur, as he worked long hours each day, building new wings, stretching Dacron sailcloth fabric over the tubing and fitting new grommets and cables to the wings. When it was time to attach the wings, Bruce Tally helped him lift the wings into place and hold them as he tied up the cables to the "King Post", the vertical tube in the center of the plane that held up the wings. It took several days and many hours of help, but they finally had the little plane ready to fly again. Despite repeated offers from Dan, Bruce steadfastly refused to be lifted off the earth within Dan's ultralight. Each time he offered, and was refused, Dan just grinned and shrugged his shoulders. But before Dan had a chance to try out his re-creation himself, his cell phone chirped. He called his boss in Chicago.

"Dan, are you ready to fly again?" said his boss. "Well, I think so. What's up?" "We have a million dollar turboprop ag plane we need to pick up. I've been in talks with the spray business that owns it, and they haven't said they definitely wouldn't give the plane back, but they haven't said they would, either. They're using it every day, as much as they can, but they're not making any payments on the plane. So I told them we would come and get it. They said if we could find it we could have it. But they continue to use it for spraying crops. I think they're moving it around, all over Southern Missouri and Northern Arkansas. You every fly one of those planes?"

Dan said no. His boss said, "Well it can't be too hard to learn to fly the darn thing, can it?" Dan said, "Well, if Superman could do it, I should be able to. Let me do some checking and I'll get back to you." After they had hung up, Dan got out his laptop and did a search for manufacturers of spray planes. When he had the one he wanted, he called and told them who he was and what he wanted. They agreed to give him a one day accelerated check out in their trainer at their factory in Texas.

He made arrangements to be there in a couple of days. His cell phone chirped again. It was from Elizabeth. She was forwarding to him a text from the Sheriff saying that three young men had been apprehended in Mississippi trying to sell stolen goods. One of which was a funny looking John Deere garden tractor with a pink hood. The sheriff didn't think the three would be coming back to Illinois for several years. In a week or two, the stolen merchandise would be returned to Illinois to be identified and picked up by their owners.

The heat coming off the west Texas plains was not quite that of a blast furnace, but it made Southern Illinois seem quite balmy in comparison. He had rented a car at the Dallas airport, and with the help of the car's GPS, drove to Olney, Texas. Olney seemed like a thousand other small towns all across the country, with brick buildings lining both sides of the main street, one stoplight controlling what little traffic there was moving thru town, and found the airport, southwest of town. Air Tractor was a sprawling complex of metal buildings that spread across half of the airport. They produced multi million dollar airplanes that would never win any beauty contests, but would endear themselves to anybody who wanted to spread or spray anything on crops such as cotton or even sow seeds by air. Their airplanes looked similar to sharks with wings, with long pointed snouts that housed super powerful jet turbine engines, turning a massive multi bladed propeller, and able to lift several tons of airplane and chemical into the air from short runways or even dirt roads or turn rows between crops.

A tall, skinny, deeply sunburned man of about fifty, welcomed Dan to Air Tractor. His name was Doug Williams, chief pilot for Air Tractor. He wore dusty jeans, scuffed boots and a cowboy shirt complete with pearled buttons. When he smiled, his grin was nearly ear to ear. "I hear you want to repossess one of our planes, eh?"

Dan said, "Yeah. So, here I am. I need to know how to fly one." "Well, it's not as hard as you think. You got any tail dragger time?" Dan explained that he had time in about a dozen different tail wheel

airplanes including the age-old Douglas DC-3. Doug smiled. "Well, now, that makes my job much easier. It's pretty late to try to start today, how about first thing tomorrow?" Dan said that would be fine. Doug said, "Great, I'll see you here ready to go at six a.m. You got a motel?" Dan said no. He motioned to one of the ladies in the office. "Lucy here can get you a good rate at the Holiday Inn Express in town." He shook Dan's hand, plucked a crumpled up cowboy hat from a coat hook by the door, then left him with Lucy.

Later that night, Dan sat on his bed and sent Elizabeth a text saying simply, 'Miss you and the boys. See you soon.' He flipped TV channels for a while, then slid under the covers and dozed off. He was afraid he would miss his wake up call but the early morning sun trying to get thru the curtains woke him up plenty early. He took a quick shower, then dressed

and ate breakfast in the lobby breakfast nook. By six o'clock he was standing outside the office at the airport, waiting for somebody to show up. He was staring out across the wide open expanse of the runway and the airport when Doug walked up behind him and nearly scared him out of his wits.

"Ready to go fly?" said Doug. "What, no ground school?" asked Dan. Doug grinned. "Maybe you are a pilot after all." He motioned Dan into the office. "Most guys can't wait to get into the hot seat." They turned down a hallway that led to a room with a simulator in it. This is where he would spend the next couple of hours. Dan tried to memorize the controls. After a break for lunch, Doug led him into a large hangar filled with about a dozen ag planes, all of them low winged monsters, mostly yellow in color, slab sided with large hoppers for holding powder or seeds or chemicals to be sprayed. One plane in particular looked different from the rest as Dan and Doug headed towards it. "This one is our trainer. I know, it looks pretty weird, but it's the only ag plane in the world with two seats. Because of that, we get pilots from all over the world coming here to train in this old girl. He patted the side of the fuselage and a hollow note rang out. She's big, and heavy and just what you need to learn on. It shouldn't take you too much time to get the hang of flying her, if you've been flying ultralights for years like you say you have. The main thing most pilots can't get used to is flying so low. We like to say, 'If you're too high to read road signs, then you're too high." Doug motioned to a lineman, who drove a tug over to the airplane, hitched onto it and pulled it out into the Texas sun. After a brief preflight, they both climbed in, Dan in the front and Doug in the seat directly behind and slightly above him. They put on helmets with built in intercoms and Doug talked Dan thru the starting procedure. When the engine had spooled up, Dan released the parking brake and the big crop duster began to roll forward. A tap on one brake or the other caused the plane to turn either left or right.

"For the first couple of flights, we'll be flying empty. After you get the hang of flying her empty, then we'll load you up with water and let you go spray some cotton fields around the airport. OK?"

Dan gave him a thumbs up signal.

They taxied to the run up area beside the runway. The turbine was incredibly easy to operate, with fewer controls than a piston engine airplane. After checking the controls, Dan was about to turn the plane around towards the runway when another plane glided over his head just a few feet higher than their plane. He instinctively ducked. Doug just grinned. "I saw him making a tight right pattern and I wondered if you'd see him. I guess you did, huh?"

"Uh, yeah, I did," Dan lied. "Does anybody around here ever use the radio?"

"Not much," said Doug. "Too busy. Enough to do without yacking to everybody else. I'll do the take off and you follow me thru on the controls. You ready?" Dan nodded. "Then let's go." Doug maneuvered the big plane onto the runway and smoothly fed in power to the turbine up front. For all the horses under the hood, the plane picked up speed slowly. When the tail came up off the ground, Doug was steering with just the rudder pedals. A few seconds later the plane lifted off. They stayed in the airport traffic pattern, with Doug letting Dan make the next few takeoffs. After that, they flew over to a nearby field of cotton, and Doug showed Dan how to make an approach to the field, after first circling the field to check on power lines or hidden pumps in the middle of the field. Only then, did Doug line up on one side of the field and dive to the edge. When it looked like they would bury the nose in the cotton, Doug hauled back on the stick and they flew across the field at over 150 mph. On the next pass, he did the same thing, except this time, he hit the spray button on the stick and evenly sprayed water on the crops as they passed overhead just three feet off the ground. At the end of the next pass, he motioned for Dan to take over. "No need to get as low as I did," said Doug. "Try for five feet or so." Dan did that smoothly. Then, they decided to take a break. While they grabbed a cup of coffee, the lineman filled the hopper with water they would spray on nearby fields. "I know you're not going to really do any spraying, that you'll just pick up the plane and deliver it back to the bank," Doug said to Dan between bites of a jelly-filled donut, " But I like to have all my students proficient in all aspects of flying these airplanes, just in case. And, you having an ultralight and being used to flying close to the ground really shows. Sometimes I have to really coax my students to get lower. They don't realize that the higher you get, the better the chances that your load of chemical will drift into other fields. That might not be a good thing if the other field is planted in something else and can't take that chemical and it kills the field." They walked back to the waiting airplane. They had left the motor running, like nearly all crop dusters do, which saves time with starting, and leaves more time in the air, working. After they had both strapped in, Doug said, "OK, now it's all yours. I won't interfere unless you're gonna kill us or something."

Dan and his instructor spent the afternoon spraying water around the airport. About three o'clock, they landed and Doug motioned for Dan to taxi over to the hangar, and park next to another spray plane painted yellow and blue. After they shut down, Doug called Dan over to the next plane. He patted the side of the plane. "This is the same plane you're going to be picking up. It's just like the one we've been flying except it only has one seat. I want you to take her around the patch a couple of times to get the feel of it, complete with full stop landings, then we'll fill it up with water and let you help out some of these poor starved for water farmers around here. OK?"

That evening, Dan closed the door to his motel room, exhausted but pleased with himself. In his flight bag was a certificate of graduation from the crop dusting school as well as a logbook endorsement from his instructor. He was ready to go get the Air Tractor spray plane.

He spent some time in the shower, getting the kinks of the day out of his tired body. After toweling off, he was thinking about supper when his cell phone buzzed. It was his boss in Chicago.

"Dan, this is a fine time to tell you this, but you can go on home. We don't need you for this job."

"Don't tell me the guy paid up?"

"No, quite the opposite," said his boss. "I'm afraid our guy crashed his plane yesterday afternoon. It seems that he didn't pull up fast enough at the end of a field, in time to clear a stand of trees. He's deceased, and the plane is totaled. So, go on home. We'll be in touch when we need you."

Dan wandered over to a steakhouse next door to the motel and ate a quiet meal by himself. After he got back to his room, he called Elizabeth and told her his plans had changed and he was coming home. She sounded like she would be happy to see him. He decided to spend the next day at his mother's house doing chores, then he called Bruce Talley and told him he'd be ready to go back to Creal Springs in two days to resume their search. The airline trip home was long and, as usual, boring.

* * * * * *

He spent the day doing odd jobs around his mom's house. She wouldn't admit it but she liked having him there. He had a feeling she was more lonely than she let on. Late that afternoon, she was upstairs putting freshly laundered underwear in his dresser when he snuck up behind her and gave her a kiss on the cheek. She tried to shoo him away but he just wrapped her up in his arms and said, "I love you mom." She said "Oh, Dan". That caused the tears to flow briefly. She wiped her eyes on the apron she always wore and hurried out of his bedroom and downstairs.

Bruce Talley answered his call on the first ring, startling Dan. "You must have had your hand hovering over the phone!" said Dan.

"Naw," said Bruce, "My well honed instincts told me you were about to call so I just picked up the phone at the right time."

Dan said a few barely audible choice words under his breath, causing Bruce to laugh.

"Well, are you fit enough to have a go at that basement in Creal Springs?" said Bruce.

"Yep. When would be a good time for you?"

"How about tomorrow morning. See you at McDonalds about 8am?"

"Is Elizabeth coming along?" asked Bruce.

"No, she has to work. It'll be just us."

"Good enough for me."

Dan said, "I'll call the lady who owns the house and let her know we'll be coming, as well as the police chief."

The next morning, they met at McDonalds. Bruce wore old jeans and a long sleeve flannel work shirt, while Dan had on jeans and a T-Shirt. Bruce said, "You're gonna get cold in a hurry down in that basement if that's all you're gonna wear."

Dan said, "I have a sweatshirt in the car. Hopefully, that's all I'll need."

They finished their breakfasts and each took a cup of coffee with them on the road to Creal Springs. They stopped briefly at the police department to let the chief know they were back in town, then continued on to the ramshackle old house on the hill above the city park where the Ozark Hotel used to stand. The chief followed them out the door.

They drove up the hill and parked next to the house and began unloading tools. The chief parked his cruiser behind theirs.

The elderly homeowner, still wearing what looked like the same faded housedress, stood along with her neighbor just outside the house, both of them with arms crossed, watching as they took picks, shovels, rope and several lanterns out of Dan's Jeep, and carried them downstairs.

"You're not forgetting what you said about fixing that cold air leak are you?" said the homeowner.

"No ma'am," said Dan. "Just as soon as we find out where that air is coming from, it will get fixed."

"I'm counting on you, young man, because I don't have the money to spare to get my basement fixed."

The chief excused himself, saying he had important city business to attend to, and left. Bruce grinned at Dan and said, "Well, that's one way to get out of dirty work."

Once again down in the musty smelling, damp basement, Dan and Bruce took turns attacking the wall with picks and sledge hammers. They had thought at first about using a hammer drill, but decided that the basement could possibly cave in from the vibrations that a heavy continuous pounding from a big drill might make. As it was, every time they hit the wall with the sledge, the rest of the house shivered as well. That made them uneasy. After all, this was an old house. So they decided to go slow, manually. When they left the house the last time, the hole was about ten inches in diameter. As they shined a flashlight thru the hole then, all they could see was blackness.

By three o'clock in the afternoon, they had enlarged the hole to about two feet in diameter. Dan couldn't stand it any longer. "I'm going to see if I can see anything on the other side of this hole. He grabbed his large flashlight, and fitted first the right leg, then his body and last, his left leg. There! He was standing on the other side of the basement wall. He couldn't quite stand up straight. The blackness was complete. A noise behind him made him swing the flashlight around just in time to see Bruce coming thru the hole. "You're not going anywhere without me, fella," he said.

"Watch your head," said Dan. "I can't stand up straight. This doesn't feel like a cave to me."

Bruce held his lantern above his head against the roof. He said, "Dan, that there is not rock, it's concrete. If I'm right, this is probably the top of the basement or whatever they called the area where the train came into." He swung his light around in a wide arc. Rubble was everywhere. He brushed past Dan and duck walked further away from the hole they had made in the wall. "Hey, look at this," Bruce said. He held up a two by four length of wood. "You don't find things like this in caves. I think we've got to be inside the hotel somewhere." The dampness quickly penetrated every part of their bodies.

He walked away from Dan, stooped over.

Bruce led the way forward, as Dan scanned his light from side to side. "Got something big and round up ahead," said Bruce. "I can't tell what it is, but I, wait a minute. Let me take another look here." Bruce was quiet for a couple of moments. Long enough for Dan to call out, "Well, what are you looking at?"

Bruce said, "I'm looking at what I believe is the smokestack from an old locomotive. It appears to me to have been knocked off the engine at some point. Come over here." Dan crawled slowly over the rubble to Bruce on his knees. "Can you see how it's tapered at the bottom and it flares out at the top?"

Dan ducked his head further and sat down beside Bruce. His lantern was beside him. Bruce started to turn away from Dan and said, "I wonder if this means that the rest of the ...." he disappeared into a hole, along with a small avalanche of dirt and rocks and rubble.

"Bruce!" yelled Dan. "Bruce! Are you all right?"

It was like he had ridden a small landslide. About ten feet down, Dan could see Bruce combing dust out of his hair with his fingers and then brushing the rest of himself off.

After a moment of silence, instead of complaining, Bruce called up to Dan, "I'm sitting on the ground next to a genuine one hundred and fifty year old locomotive. I think we've just found your train." Dan started over the side but Bruce stopped him. Bruce said, "Wait! Don't come down here. We need a ladder or something. I'm going to try to climb up the side of the engine to get out of this hole. Grab me when you can."

Dan helped Bruce out of the hole, and they made their way back into the basement thru the hole they had created.

They were hot, tired and sweaty, so they decided to knock it off until tomorrow. They covered the hole with a tarp and moved the shelves back against the wall to hold the tarp in place.

Dan said "When we come back tomorrow, we need to bring Elizabeth so she can be in on this. And we need to bring a ladder."

Bruce agreed.

That evening after supper, While the boys were outside playing, Dan took Elizabeth's hands and looked her in the eye and said, "I am not a miracle worker. I am not a magician. I can't conjure up things from the past, but sometimes, just sometimes, I do get lucky."

She stared into his soft brown eyes and said, "That's a pretty big disclaimer, buster. What gives?"

"I think we found the train," Dan said softly.

Elizabeth again just stared into his big brown eyes for a moment, then the tears started. "Oh my god, oh my god, are you really sure. I mean, really, really sure?"

Dan said, "Well, we found A train. How's that for starters?"

She said, Did you look, I mean, was there any, I, well..is..."

Dan put his finger on her lips. "We haven't looked inside it yet. Bruce and I plan to do that tomorrow. You want to come along?

"You bet I do!" She almost shouted. The she became subdued again. "After all these years. My grandmother could know for sure about her father, my great grandfather. Wow."

Dan said, "Let's not jump to conclusions just yet. Keep an open mind, ok? Things may not turn out how you wish them to. It's just that, well, we don't know. But we will, tomorrow, I hope.

Pick you up at seven?"

Chapter Twenty-Six

The next day started at McDonalds just like yesterday. They were a little more subdued, since they had found the train. Fortunately, nobody asked them any questions today. They finished breakfast, then climbed into Dan's Jeep with the ladder strapped onto the roof, and once again drove down to Creal Springs.

And, once again, the two old ladies were standing outside on the lawn when they pulled in. The homeowner said, "Well, have you found anything yet?"

Dan said, "We're exploring a small cave on the other side of your basement wall. We should be done in a day or two and then you'll get your wall sealed up and you won't have any more cold drafts of air to worry about." The old lady seemed pleased with that, and they headed for her neighbor's house. No use standing around outside with nobody else to talk to.

Dan moved the shelves away from the hole in the wall, and slipped thru the opening to the other side. He helped Elizabeth thru, then offered Bruce a hand. Bruce waved his hand away and put one leg, then the other thru until he was standing with Dan and Elizabeth. They picked up their flashlights and headed for the hole in the rubble that Bruce had fallen thru. Bruce had thought to bring a short shovel with him to move rocks and debris with. He dropped into the hole first, then made sure the other two could fit alongside him. Then he turned his body around and slid behind the second big rear drive wheel. He shined his flashlight back toward the coal tender and said, "It looks pretty good to me. Very little rubble to move away. I think we can make it quite a way by crawling under the cars." Bruce used his shovel to move rocks and other debris away from under the couplers, creating a small tunnel they could squeeze thru to get to the rear of the train.

Elizabeth went next under the locomotive, then Dan. The locomotive was built a scant fifteen inches off the ground. Careful not to bang their heads on the low slung engine, all three slid on their bellies slowly under the locomotive, then the coal car, and finally a Pullman style coach. It had higher clearance from the tracks so they could actually sit up under it. Barely.

The problem was getting into the Pullman car. When the roof over the train collapsed, tons of bricks, concrete and dirt, plus huge wooden beams dropped straight down onto the train, covering it up. The open spaces between each car where they were coupled together was mounded up with debris that reached higher than the roof of the Pullman as well as the locomotive and tender. There was no way they could get into the Pullman thru the doors on each end. They were underneath the Pullman, but how to get into the car?

Dan lay on his back under the car and kicked upward at the floor with both feet. Nothing happened. Bruce studied the underside of the car. He wasn't ready to admit defeat but he couldn't see any other way than to go back to town and buy or rent a battery operated sawsall and cut thru the floor.

Then Elizabeth said, "Hey I found a hole in the floor!"

They crawled over to the rear of the Pullman and looked at what she had found. Dan looked at Bruce and they both grinned. They started laughing. Elizabeth looked at each of them and said, "What's so funny?"

Bruce said, "Dan, you tell her."

Dan said, "Honey, this may be the only time in your life that you get to look at a toilet from the other end." The guys both roared with laughter. She got a pouty look on her face, then broke into laughter, too. "This is a toilet?"

Bruce said yes, that toilets on the railroad cars in the old days dumped directly onto the tracks, because the trains had no holding tanks. That caused her to instantly turn over and look at the track she was resting on.

Bruce looked at the toilet again, with a thoughtful look on his face. "Dan, that toilet looks like it is made out of metal, maybe aluminum. It should be lighter than porcelain, so why don't you try and see if you can push it up with your feet. I see screw holes around the base of the toilet, and I'll bet that it's not fastened down too tight. It's worth a try."

Dan moved himself under the toilet and kicked upwards once, twice then several more times. He rested his legs a moment. Then he said, "Bruce why don't you get next to me and let's both try to move that toilet. The toilet moved some, but not enough. Then Elizabeth lay down and the three of them kicked and strained their legs. POP! The toilet flew upward with a bang and they were looking at the inside of the bathroom from below.

Elizabeth carefully stood up in the hole made by the toilet. She hoisted herself up into the bathroom. "I'd invite you guys to join me, but there's no room for more than one person." She looked around and found the door. "I'll step out of here and you guys can come up one at a time." She tried the doorknob and found that it opened easily; then she stepped out of the bathroom. Dan hoisted himself up into the little room next; then stepped out so Bruce could come up. Bruce looked around at the tiny 'facilities' then opened the door and stepped out into the main room of the coach, to find Dan staring intently at Elizabeth who was standing stock still, staring across the room.

Her eyes were riveted on the mummified body of a man sitting on the floor in front of a huge safe. He was dressed in corduroy pants and shirt, and wearing a leather vest with a badge pinned to it. His revolver was in his hand. The safe had WELLS FARGO imprinted in gold leaf across the front of the safe door.

The silence was deafening. "That's my great-grandfather," she whispered.

Bruce and Dan said nothing. They let her have a few moments to herself, standing there. Finally, she moved across the room towards her great-grandfather. Only then, did they notice the other two dead men in the room, both near the back wall next to the toilet. They were sprawled behind the pot-bellied stove, which bore several shiny nicks created by bullets from her great-grandfathers gun. They shot him, and he had shot them.

They all sat down, Elizabeth on the swivel chair at an old roll top desk, Dan and Bruce on a bench that ran along one wall of the car.

"Now what?" asked Dan, looking at Elizabeth.

"I have no idea what to do about all of this," said Elizabeth.

Bruce cleared his throat. He looked at her then Dan. "This is really none of my business, but, I would like to give you both my two cents worth, if I may."

They both nodded.

Bruce said, "This train disappeared almost a hundred years ago. You," he nodded at Elizabeth, "Have the money these robbers were trying to get at." She gulped and nodded again, her eyes downcast towards her great-grandfather.

"The money that caused my great-grandfather to be killed over."

Bruce said, "That part doesn't matter. Even if the bandits had gotten the money, he would have been killed anyway. See what I mean?"

"What I would like to suggest is, this train was never found. We didn't find it, either.

Here's why. Let's say we announce to the world that we found a long lost payroll train. First thing is, Somebody is going to want to dig up this train. So there's two old ladies up top who are going to lose their homes, they'll have to move because somebody is going to want to tear down their homes to dig up this train. They don't look like they have more than two nickels to rub together. All this hullabaloo might make them homeless. When they start investigating all this, they are going to want to know why you didn't give the money back to, to...whomever! Why did you keep it?"

Elizabeth said, "Well, old Howard Bailey told me that all of the principles in this robbery are dead. The coal companies are out of business, all the people involved are long dead, so who benefits? He told me to keep the money and use it for something good."

Bruce said, "He's one hundred percent right. I agree with him. I think you should use it for, for...your boys' college education.

I think, given the circumstances, your great-grandfather would probably agree, too. Wells Fargo wrote off that money almost a hundred years ago. The miners all got paid, so they aren't entitled to any of it. Why create a big stink if you don't have to?

As far as I'm concerned, we are sitting inside a gravesite. I say we take a last look around and back out of here, and go up top and fix the hole in that lady's basement and we're done. Anybody asks, we never found the train. It was a wild goose chase."

Dan said. "Sounds good to me. Elizabeth?"

She let out a big sigh. "You guys are both right. It's just, after all this time, and now we've found him, and we're just going to walk away. What do I tell my grandmother?"

Dan said, "Give her his badge. Explain what we've been talking about. I think she'll say we all did the right thing, and she'll know her daddy

156

died doing the right thing, defending his company from the bad guys, right until the very end. I think that's a fitting tribute."

She walked over to her great grandfather's body, kneeled down and stroked his vest, then unpinned his badge and put it in her pocket.

"Goodbye great-grandpa," she said. She stood up and walked by to the bathroom, and let herself down under the car, followed by Bruce and Dan.

It was nearly suppertime before the three of them finished patching the hole in the basement wall. When the old ladies wanted to know what was causing the cold air, Bruce told her it was an underground cave that was too small for them to follow.

A few nights later, Dan and Elizabeth sat on the front porch. Supper had been good, with hamburgers cooked on the grill in the backyard, and corn on the cobb and potatoes.

The boys were working off their remaining energy by chasing each other around the trees in the front yard, yelling and laughing and having fun.

Elizabeth and Dan rocked the swing slightly back and forth. She said, "It can't get much better than this, you know?"

Dan said, "Well, I think it could get a little better."

"Oh? How?"

"Well, I think we should get a dog for the boys."

"A dog, huh?"

"Yeah. Something not too big, with curly hair. Sort of like Benji, in the movies."

"Uh, a moment ago, you said 'we'. That implies you and me, and that sounds like you have become a part of this family."

157

"Yeah, well, I was going to get around to that. Will you marry me?"

Elizabeth jumped up off the swing, *"yes! yes! yes!"*

The boys stopped playing and Mason said, "Hey, what's all the yelling about?"

Elizabeth said, "We're gonna get a dog!"

This book is entirely fiction. However, The Ozark Hotel in Creal Springs, IL. was real, and was a beautiful hotel. And, Charles Lindbergh really did land near Carterville during his barnstorming days, just before he crossed the Atlantic. Southern Illinois is full of history. Did you know that hundreds of paddlewheel steamboats were built along the Ohio near Cairo? That might become part of the story in another book....

35340998R00098

Made in the USA
Columbia, SC
20 November 2018